THE VILEST TRASH EVER TO COME
OUT OF THE CONFEDERACY . . .

"The folks around here are well acquainted with the Halseys."

Slocum said, "What is it they do up there?"

"Run cattle, a few horses. Or that's what they'll tell you if you come asking. But if there's a stage robbery within fifty miles, or a bank job in Denver or Colorado Springs, or a dead man found in a gully with his pockets turned out, you can figure they probably had a hand in it. If you're going up after them, you be careful. They swarm like bees. They'll pick the flesh off your bones."

DON'T MISS THESE
ALL-ACTION WESTERN SERIES
FROM THE BERKLEY PUBLISHING GROUP

THE GUNSMITH by J. R. Roberts
Clint Adams was a legend among lawmen, outlaws, and
ladies. They called him . . . the Gunsmith.

LONGARM by Tabor Evans
The popular long-running series about U.S. Deputy Marshal
Long—his life, his loves, his fight for justice.

LONE STAR by Wesley Ellis
The blazing adventures of Jessica Starbuck and the martial
arts master, Ki. Over eight million copies in print.

SLOCUM by Jake Logan
Today's longest-running action western. John Slocum rides
a deadly trail of hot blood and cold steel.

JAKE LOGAN

BLOOD FEVER

BERKLEY BOOKS, NEW YORK

BLOOD FEVER

A Berkley Book / published by arrangement with
the author

PRINTING HISTORY
Berkley edition / December 1992

ISBN: 0-425-13532-2

A BERKLEY BOOK ® TM 757,375
Berkley Books are published by The Berkley Publishing Group,
200 Madison Avenue, New York, New York 10016.
The name "Berkley" and the "B" logo
are trademarks belonging to Berkley Publishing Corporation.

PRINTED IN THE UNITED STATES OF AMERICA

10 9 8 7 6 5 4 3 2 1

1

They were confident because there were two of them.

Maybe he looked like an easy mark in the darkness between the saddler's shop and the livery. Slocum had rolled and lighted a cigarette, and the flare of the match had barely faded from his eyes when they were there, one in front and one behind, blocking easy escape. The one in front was worked up for it, breathing hard, as if he'd run a long way to get there in time.

Only a sliver of moon, making them scarcely more than shapes in the black. Slocum could smell them, the musty and rank odor of old sweat and wood smoke and horse manure. When the man in front grinned, the lamplight from the saloon up the street gleamed against his wet teeth.

"Say, mister," he said, "you got an extra cigar on you?"

A southern accent. The Carolinas, or maybe Tennessee. Slocum stepped edgeways, hoping to bring both of them into his line of sight. They advanced on him accordingly, closing the gap to something less than ten feet, either side.

The second man said, "He ain't talking, Rory. Maybe he don't smoke cigars." A younger voice, thinner, with the keening edge of tension.

Rory snapped, "Don't say names, you goddamned crackerhead!"

"You boys got business with me, state what it is," Slocum said. "Otherwise move on."

"A cocky one," Rory said. "Gonna make it tough on us. You was pretty cocky at that faro table this evening, too. Winning big, it looked like to me."

"If you'd hung around long enough you'd have seen me lose big. You're tapping an empty hole."

"Maybe, maybe not," Rory said. All false amiability was gone from his voice now. "You just shell out and we'll see."

There it was. Slocum tensed, waiting for the move that would open the ball. It could be they'd done this a hundred times before, or it could be this was the first time; either way they'd have the motions worked out— a shove from one to put him off balance and then from the other a thrust with a knife or a pistol barrel.

It was fast. Rory jerked to the right, a flitting shadow. Slocum saw the glint of metal. The second man lunged toward him, arms coming up. Slocum kicked hard with his left foot, felt it connect, heard the man grunt with surprise and pain. In the same instant he whipped his pistol from its holster, a .36 Navy Colt, cocking it on the rise.

Rory saw it coming too late and tried to turn away as Slocum fired. The muzzle blast illuminated a blocky, chinless face with grizzled beard stubble and thick eyebrows arched in terror, and mixed with the roar of the explosion was the slap of a pistol ball against flesh.

Rory screamed, a high-pitched, wavering shriek.

Slocum dove to the left, swinging the pistol toward the second man. But the man had already turned tail and was running, the ching of his spurs loud in the clear air. There was the quick rattle of boot soles against wood as he crossed the boardwalk down the street, and then he was gone.

Up the street, the forms of curious men appeared against the slatted light of the saloon doors.

"Somebody fetch a lantern!" Slocum hollered. "You got a man on the ground here!"

Rory lay with his mouth open, breathing at a fast, doggish pant against the pain. In a moment a figure came hurrying from the porch with a lantern, the yellow glow shooting long shadows against the blank sides of the buildings that lined the street. It was the bartender from the saloon, in his shirtsleeves and smudged apron. He came to Slocum and the fallen man and crouched down with the lantern, saying nothing.

Arm wound, just above the elbow, the blood flowing and bright red, soaking through the dirty fabric of Rory's shirt. Beside him on the ground lay a hunting knife with a six inch blade. The bartender reached for it. Slocum, still standing, nudged the man's hand away with the toe of his boot.

"Leave it."

Now that it was safe, the crowd from the saloon porch came down to gawk. They mumbled among themselves, a half dozen men jostling each other in the small circle of lantern light, asking pointless questions. Someone gave a low whistle of surprise.

"Rory Halsey, big as life," one of them said.

"He'll lose that arm," another added.

Slocum said, "You got a lawman here, somebody better fetch him. And a doctor."

"He won't take to no town doctor," a man said.

One of the crowd trotted off down the street, in the direction of the Gold Dollar, a larger, fancier saloon and gambling hall. Slocum stood and waited, ignoring questions from the rest of them, his pistol holstered now and his arms crossed over his chest. Blood and shooting always drew a crowd. They came to stare and shake their heads, and congratulate themselves that somebody else had died and they were still here.

In a few minutes the marshal arrived, a young man in a broad, flat-brimmed hat and a frock coat that smelled of cigar smoke and whiskey. His shoulder-length hair gleamed in the lantern light, and his mustache was neatly trimmed. He carried his two Army Colts in a red sash, butts forward, after the fashion of Bill Hickok. His eyes were disapproving, small and widely set.

He looked at the wounded man. His mouth set hard when he saw the knife on the ground. He stared at Slocum, eyes narrowed. "What happened?"

"I shot him."

"I see that. You have a reason?"

Slocum told it.

The Marshal said nothing for a moment. Then, "You say there was two of them. Where's the other one?"

"Run off. You might want to think about fetching a doctor. This man's bleeding all over your nice clean street."

The Marshal gave him a hard, appraising glare, taking in the full six feet of Slocum's bulk, the wide shoulders and the pistol slung low on his hip. Measuring him, weighing him as a threat. Slocum had felt the rake of the same stare a hundred times before, and he had seen men die when they misjudged what they saw.

The Marshal said, calmly, "Dobbs, get a couple of boys and take Rory to my office. I'll see he gets treated. Anybody seen Deward in town tonight?"

"He didn't come in, Reed," someone answered. "Just Rory and Tyson. They said Deward was home sitting up with the old man."

They watched as the bartender and two others hoisted the wounded man and carried him away. Marshal Reed said to Slocum, "What's your name, mister?"

"John Slocum."

"Could be I've heard of you."

"Could be."

"You know who this man is you shot?"

"I know what he is. That's enough."

Reed took a deep breath. He put his hands behind him, pulling the coat back from the twin walnut grips of his revolvers. "You tell it pretty plain, and there's the knife on the ground, and Rory don't have nobody here to vouch for him. I guess there's nothing I can hold you for. You been in Colorado long?"

"Passing through."

"You planning to take your time, or are you in a hurry?"

"Are you asking me or telling me?"

Reed snorted. He curled his lip. "Things can get ugly when something like this happens. Lots of family bitterness, if you get my meaning."

"Anybody wants to see me about this, I'm right here."

"If Deward wants to see you, he'll find you. I'd just as soon it was someplace other than here."

"And who's Deward?"

Reed said nothing for a moment. Then, "A man who might take an interest."

Slocum had planned on heading out in the morning. He had received a telegram in Santa Fe telling him his services were needed by a cattleman's association in the Powder River country of Wyoming. People were waiting on him. Though some could take his departure as a sign of weakness, as cowardice, he did not feel inclined to explain himself.

He said, "Marshal, when I leave here, which will be when I feel like it, I'll be riding north. Anybody comes asking about it, you tell them that."

His horse went lame just before noon.

The near foreleg. Slocum bent the hoof up and looked at the splotch of dark color next to the frog. A stone bruise. He dropped the hoof, cursed, then straightened and looked around him.

He was on a high sagebrush plateau, tablelands, with the foothills hard to the west and beyond them the purpled vastness of the mountains. About ten miles north of Garrison. There were towns ahead of him somewhere, but he was uncertain just how far. Denver was at least two days' ride. His best bet would be to find a ranch and make a trade. He had three hundred dollars in gold coin in his saddlebags, faro winnings, the result of a winter spent in the gambling halls in Santa Fe and Albuquerque.

He set out on foot, leading the limping horse, cursing his late start. He had taken his time about leaving Garrison this morning, making himself highly visible in case anyone wanted to initiate trouble over last night's shooting. No one had. Nor had anyone gone out of his way to be friendly to him, or even to be seen standing next to him. Nice neighborly little town, Garrison, Colorado. Slocum was glad to have put it behind him.

In an hour he saw the smoke of a camp.

The tablelands broke here, rolling off to the east toward the plains, and there was the green of willows marking the course of a creek running down out of the mountains. A stand of cottonwoods stood at the bottom of a small swale, and the smoke rose from the middle of it, a straight, thin line in the air. Slocum approached it warily, leaving his horse on the back side of a small, treeless ridge. He crested the rise quickly and crouched in the sage to have a look.

He saw horses, picketed out in the flat beyond the creek.

Two wagons. One with a canvas top like an old prairie schooner, the other a cook's rig with an open box end. Two large white tents were set side by side, and a thin man tended a pot hung from crossed rods set up over the fire. He had a shock of white hair.

Not buffalo hunters. The camp looked too clean and orderly. Slocum saw nothing ominous, and he was afoot. He smelled coffee, and that settled it for him.

He fetched his horse and hailed the camp. The cook waved him in, then with his hands on his rail-thin hips, stood and watched Slocum come down. He was ancient, with a scraggly, tobacco-stained beard.

"Glad to see you," he called. "Be a pleasure to gab at an intelligent man for a damn change. Have a cup of coffee. There'll be grub in a little bit."

He poured the coffee while Slocum tied his horse and stripped the saddle and blankets from its back. The cook handed him the cup and told Slocum his name was Silas and his boss's name was Mr. Amos Creede, the famous scout, and they'd been out a week from Denver and he was drove damn near crazy.

"Dudes," he said. "Come out from Chicago to get themselves some antelope and some deer and maybe a bear. Green as gourds, all three of them, though the woman is a looker. Where you from?"

Silas inspected the stone bruise, shaking his head at Slocum's hard luck. "We got a couple extra in the remuda," Silas said. "Most likely Mr. Creede will make a deal with you. He's due in here anytime."

Slocum passed a pleasant ten minutes, sipping the strong coffee and listening to Silas rant and rail about the trials of camping with rich Easterners. They heard horses trumpet, and a few minutes later Mr. Creede rode in with his customers tagging along behind him.

Creede was small, nearly as old as Silas, a wrinkled little whipsaw of a man in stained buckskins and a wide-brimmed hat. He nodded once to Slocum, then he and his three customers dismounted. Creede took the horses and tied them to a picket line strung between the trees. His customers stood near the tents and beat the dust from their clothes, and one of them was sure enough a woman.

Slim, compact, in a tight riding skirt and high boots, both of the finest material. She wore a short-brimmed hat with a red scarf, and she removed this and her hair fell, cascading down her back. It was dark hair, as black as Slocum's own, with a blazing streak of white down the center. She was young, not more than twenty-five, her cheekbones high and prominent. She looked at Slocum, nodded once, and retired to her tent.

"Lord have mercy," Slocum breathed.

Silas whispered, "What'd I tell you?"

The other two customers finished dusting themselves off and stepped forward. Howard Conway was a portly man with a small, well-trimmed mustache. His soft round face was sizzled red from his week under the Colorado sun. He wore range clothes and suspenders, but still looked as if he were in blue serge. Beside him was a younger man, younger than the girl, a lanky kid Conway introduced as his nephew, Nathan. Nathan had a sneer that looked as if it were a permanent fixture. They both carried new long-barreled hunting rifles, and Mr. Conway handed Nathan his to take away.

"Heading for Denver, Mr. Slocum?"

"North, more or less."

"Cowboy, are you? Range rider?"

"Among other things."

They spoke of the hunting. So far the results had been poor, Mr. Conway said, but he was hopeful. Slocum found him outwardly pleasant, but with a strange, tight undercurrent of suspicion—and something else that Slocum could not quite put his finger on. Something bitter.

Nathan joined them. He sneered, "Reason we haven't seen any game is that old man isn't half the scout he's made out to be."

"Now, Nathan, your manners," Conway said.

"I didn't come all the way out here to practice my manners. I came to shoot antelope, but this old fool can't seem to find any."

The woman emerged from the tent. She had changed from her riding clothes into a full skirt and plain cotton blouse. Her hair was pulled back into a bun, and the tightness of it against her head made the streak of white seem even more prominent.

Conway said, "This is my daughter, Julia."

Slocum touched his hat brim. She regarded him with a full, open look, making no pretense of modesty. A striking woman, with a pleasing swell of hip below a tiny waist he'd bet he could circle with his two hands. Her breasts were high and round, her posture almost a challenge. Slocum felt himself stir—uselessly; he'd be away and gone in an hour.

"It looks as if lunch is nearly ready," she said. Her voice was deep and smoky. "Perhaps you could join us."

Slocum touched his hat brim once again. "Love to," he said.

Lunch was stew and coffee. Slocum sat cross-legged near the fire, holding his plate; the three Easterners had folding canvas chairs and ate with their plates balanced in their laps. Nathan hunkered over his food, looking resentful and angry with the world in general. Mr. Conway made small talk. He praised the beauty of the high plains country, the vastness of the mountains that towered over them and the clear, thin air.

Slocum looked up twice and found Julia staring at him. Each time, she moved her eyes away, but she was in no hurry to do so. The hint of a smile played around the corners of her mouth.

Silas and Creede both ate standing up next to the cook wagon. Creede, squint-eyed and brooding, told Slocum he could look over the extra horses in the remuda after lunch, and they'd work a trade. Slocum thanked him. He had nearly finished his meal when he saw dust rising in the air to the southwest.

He scraped his plate into the fire and tossed it into the wash pot. He looked at Creede. "You got field glasses?"

Creede did not speak. Apparently he had seen the

dust as well. He reached behind him in the wagon and brought out a tarnished brass telescope. Slocum took it and started up the slope.

"What is it?" Conway called after him.

"Hard to say," Slocum told him. "I'll take a look."

He climbed to the crest of the hill, hunkered down near the rocks and trained the scope on the dust cloud.

Six or maybe eight riders. Hard to tell for sure from the way they were bunched up. No more than half a mile away, heading at a steady trot directly toward the smoke of the camp.

He cursed. He'd known there was a chance they would come. Had it not been for his horse laming up, he'd be out in open country and could make a run for it, and innocent people would not be involved. He came back down the slope to the fire.

"Mr. Conway, you'll want to get your daughter into the tent."

"What are you talking about?"

"We're about to have visitors. It's probably best they don't see her."

2

Julia rose and without a word walked to her tent and disappeared inside. Mr. Conway watched her go, then frowned at Slocum, as if puzzled by the urgency in his voice.

"Get behind the wagons and stay there," Slocum said.

Creede and Silas moved at once, Silas pausing to yank a rifle from the open box of the cook wagon. Mr. Conway and his nephew stood up, but made no attempt to take cover. Slocum drew his pistol, stepped to them and gave Nathan a push. "Go!" he shouted. "Now!"

"Get your hands away from me!" Nathan said. He squared off, fists clenched. Slocum gave him another shove, harder this time, and Silas grabbed the boy by the collar and pulled him behind the wagon. Mr. Conway, seeing the way of it, joined them with no more shoving required.

"I don't know what this is about or what you think you're doing," he said, "but you'd better have a good reason for it. When I speak to the sheriff in Denver—"

"Shut up," Silas said. "Get down and keep down." He looked at Slocum. "How you want to handle it?"

"Don't do anything. I'm the one they're after."

"Look yonder," Creede said. "Getting around us."

Slocum looked. Three men had appeared on the hill behind them, all with rifles drawn.

He cursed.

Five riders now topped the rise in front of them, and rode down the slope at an easy walk. A hard-looking bunch: wide-brimmed, shapeless hats, lean faces bristled with stubble or thick mustaches. Most were booted and spurred. Pistol belts were strapped on over jackets, and one man had a pair of crossed bandoleers.

Two of them had their rifles pulled, with the barrels up, stocks planted against their thighs.

In the center was a big man with a tangled Abe Lincoln beard and no mustache, his chest and belly straining the buttons of his shirt. His mouth was open, showing one tooth broken off even at the gum line, and the others straight and yellowed the color of old piano keys. As he drew closer, Slocum counted at least three revolvers on him, two in belt holsters and the other tucked into his pants.

The riders spread out across the slope, so as not to offer a bunched target. Halted there. Horses snorted and curb chains jingled.

"This is a peaceful camp!" Slocum called. "State your intentions!"

The big man in the middle spoke. "One of you is named Slocum," he said. His voice was harsh and deep and rasping. "I imagine that's you, doing the talking. You want to keep it peaceful, step out here."

"I like it fine where I am."

The man nodded, as if weary, but resigned to difficulties. "We can do it that way, if you want. Just takes longer. More people likely to get hurt."

Silas cocked his rifle. "You boys just move on. You got no right to come in here all weapon heavy and cause trouble."

"Be smart about this," the leader said. "You got three rifles on the hill behind you, another couple up here. It comes to a shoot, y'all ain't going to do too well."

"It comes to a shoot, you're the first one we take down," Slocum said.

"And then you all die."

The man sat back in the saddle, crossed his arms over his chest and waited.

Slocum said, "These people got no part in it."

"Then suppose you keep from causing them grief, and step out here."

Slocum moved out from the wagon, his pistol held low down by his side. His thumb was on the hammer. "I'm Slocum," he said.

"Lay the gun down."

He hesitated, then let the pistol fall from his grip.

"The rest of you step out and shuck your iron," the leader said.

Slowly the four men stepped out from the wagon, and the three riders from the hill behind them rode in to join the rest. Silas tossed his rifle down, leaned forward and spat.

"On the ground. Sit down and stay there," the big man said. He looked to his left and then to his right. "Bring him to me."

The two riders on either side of him swung down. One was a smaller, leaner version of the leader, but chinless without the beard. His eyes were small and malicious. The other, the one wearing the bandoleers, was a larger man. He was red-haired, with a thick chest and a wide, round face.

They came up to Slocum, and each grabbed an arm. Slocum shoved them away, and the big man reached up and took a handful of Slocum's shirt. The smaller man drew his pistol and dug the barrel into the small of Slocum's back.

"I'll blow you in half, just as soon as not," the man growled.

They pushed him forward, until he stood directly before the bearded leader.

"My name is Deward Halsey," the bearded man said. "They tell me you met my brother Rory last night."

Slocum said nothing.

"They're going to have to cut off the arm," Deward said. "Hell of a waste. He was a good rifle shot."

"He called it," Slocum said.

Deward nodded. "Maybe so. But now I'm calling this one." He looked at the smaller man beside Slocum. "Bobby Todd," he said. "The kid from Texas. Remember?"

"The mouthy one," Bobby Todd said. "The one we put the mark on."

"That's the one. Same thing for him."

Slocum turned as Bobby Todd reached out to grab his arm once more. He jerked away, taking a step back, and Bobby Todd hit him in the jaw, a glancing blow that did not hurt him but caused him to stumble back a few more feet. Bobby Todd came after him, ready to give him another.

Slocum came in with his right fist—a solid blow just under the cheekbone that snapped Bobby Todd's head back, smashing lips against teeth—and then the left, catching him as he fell. And then the man with the bandoleers was on Slocum, grabbing him, pinning his arms behind his back. Laughing.

Bobby Todd pushed himself into a sitting position and put fingers to his busted lip. "Be a son of a bitch," he said. He placed his hands on the ground to support himself as he got to his feet, and without taking his eyes from Slocum, he said, "Hold him, Hoffman. Hold him good and tight."

It was coming. The man behind Slocum, Hoffman, shifted mechanically, bracing against Slocum with his feet planted wide. Slocum tensed the muscles of his stomach, ready for it. Bobby Todd was plainly rattled, blood seeping from his smashed lip and his jaw hanging slack, showing yellowed teeth.

Bobby Todd snarled and lunged forward, driving a fist into Slocum's belly. Slocum's breath spewed out between clenched teeth, and he twisted sideways, but Hoffman held him upright and Bobby Todd slammed into him again, putting his whole body into it, grunting with the effort. Slocum raged against Hoffman's arms. A blow to the face blinded him for a second, and he bared his teeth like a cornered animal. He lashed out with a boot, feeling the heel connect with Bobby Todd's leg, thigh, something—*good*— and then Hoffman brought up a thick forearm and hooked it under Slocum's jaw, bending him backward and choking off his breath. Bobby Todd hit him twice more, shuddering blows, and then Slocum was smelling Bobby Todd's sour breath, and a knee smashed into his groin. He folded inward, his wind leaving him completely and his mouth jerking open in a silent scream.

He was on the ground, and a boot thudded into his ribs, then another. He heard a voice—the kid's voice, Nathan, and that surprised him—"For Christ's sake stop it!"

Deward said, "Stand where you are, boy—"

Slocum heard the scramble of feet, then one gunshot. A grunt of pain. He rolled over, and through a haze saw Nathan on the ground in front of the fire, his hands clutching at his thigh where blood seeped through his fingers. Beside him was the rifle Silas had dropped.

A scream, and then Julia burst from the tent and flung herself down beside Nathan.

Mr. Conway shouted, "Julia, no!" He started for her. One of the mounted men spurred forward and cut him off, pistol drawn.

Deward said, "Bobby Todd. The girl—look at her!"

Bobby Todd, panting from the exertion, with his arm raised to wipe the blood from his chin, turned. Slocum saw him jerk, as if from a physical blow, when he caught sight of Julia.

"Jesus Christ, Deward. Just like the old woman said. White mark in her hair and everything." He looked from the girl to Deward and back again.

"Our lucky day," Deward said. "Tyson! See to the girl!"

"You keep your hands off her!" Conway screamed.

He was ignored. Another man, taller, but also obvious kin to the bearded Deward, dismounted and moved to where Julia knelt. He reached for her arm and she jerked away. Nathan spat something at him, and the man turned and kicked him once in the face. He grabbed for Julia again, caught her by the arm and jerked her roughly to her feet. She struggled, and the man raised his hand as if to strike her. She flinched away.

Deward said, "Don't mark her!"

"Leave her alone!" Conway shouted, his voice breaking. "Get away from her!" He tried to move around the mounted man in front of him, but the man brandished his pistol once more, and Conway stepped back.

Deward raised a hand and pointed at him. "You people been lucky so far. You best hold still. This your woman?"

"She's my daughter."

"Well," Deward said, "we're taking her. We won't keep her long, maybe two days at most. She has something important she's got to tend to for us, and then we'll bring her back and drop her somewhere near town."

"Oh, God," Conway said. His face was slack with horror, and Slocum could imagine the things flashing through his mind.

He gathered himself. The pain was loosening and he could move; it was still a physical presence, but bearable, and he could taste the salt of blood in his mouth, but he was alive. Hoffman was behind him, over him. He could feel the toes of the man's boots against his back. He took a deep breath and rolled.

Hoffman pitched forward with a shout, hit the ground heavily, grunting. Then, strangely, he laughed again, as if pleased at this. Slocum was up and waiting as the man got to his hands and knees. He swung a boot and kicked him just below the ear. Hoffman grunted again, and flicked his head sideways, as if at a fly, then lumbered the rest of the way to his feet. He was still grinning, six and a half feet tall with a broad,

...ace and small, pig-looking eyes, the thick arms below the rolled sleeves of his shirt covered with fine orange hair.

Bobby Todd picked up the rifle from next to the wounded Nathan and turned it on Slocum. He levered a shell into the chamber. "Let me cut him down, Deward. Real quick and clean."

"No," Deward said. "Do it right." He looked around him. "Couple of you boys jump down and see to the fire. Let's get it finished."

Two of the others dismounted and began gathering fuel, clumps of dead sage and dried buffalo chips and wood from the back of the cook wagon. They piled it onto the cook fire, one of them knocking over the iron frame for the coffeepot.

Hoffman leered at Slocum. "Hey," he said. "The last time the guy bawled like a calf. You think this one will?"

"Maybe he ought to be tied like a calf, too," Bobby Todd said. He grabbed a grass rope from the nearest horse. He gave the rifle to the man holding Julia, then approached Slocum.

He played out a small, fist-sized loop. "Hold out your hands."

Slocum lunged, catching Bobby Todd around the waist and pushing him over. Bobby Todd cried out and went down, Slocum's shoulder plowing into his belly. Slocum rolled off him, dove for the pile of firewood and grabbed a length of it. He turned on his knees as Bobby Todd came for him. He smashed it into the man's face and saw the blood gush as the man fell back with a shout of pain.

Hoffman was on him, one huge hand swinging down to catch Slocum alongside the head, nearly jarring his wits loose. The piece of wood flew useless from his hand, and as he went down, the two others were there. Someone kicked him on the shoulder, hard, another boot glanced off his neck, and he felt the sharp rowel of a spur rake across his forehead. Then Hoffman jerked him to his feet, and Bobby Todd was pounding into him, the spittle spraying from his open mouth as he hammered again and again.

"This boy's a little tough," Hoffman said. He hooked a leg under Slocum's feet and put him down. In an instant the other two men were on him, each taking an arm, pinning him to the ground, Hoffman sitting on his legs, laughing again.

"We'll see how goddamned tough he is," Bobby Todd said. He went to his horse and untied something from behind his saddle, brought it back.

A short running iron. He stuffed it deep into the coals of the fire.

Slocum felt the dirt and gravel tearing into his cheek. He strained, but the two men on his arms had him nailed to the ground.

"People got to learn," Deward said. Up there on his horse he sounded far away. "You don't draw blood from a Halsey and then walk away from it unmarked. The rest of you watch this, and tell people what you seen."

Slocum struggled, uselessly. His head was turned to where he could see the fire, see Bobby Todd walk back to it, crouch down next to it, see him pull on a leather glove. He saw the running iron come out, the tip of it a pulsing red. Bobby Todd spat on it and it sizzled, and he turned to look down at Slocum and grinned.

He stood, the iron in his hand.

"For God's sake, stop this." Conway's voice, thin and shaking.

"You watch," Deward said. "You watch and tell people what happens to anyone crosses us."

"Where do you want it?" Bobby Todd said.

"The face," Deward said. "Left cheek, so everybody can see it."

"Turn him over so I can get to his face," Bobby Todd directed.

Slocum felt the pressure on his arms and legs ease as the men shifted, preparing to turn him over. It was enough. He surged, broke his right arm free, rolled and came up swinging. He smashed his fist into someone's face and saw him go reeling back.

Hoffman reached forward and grabbed Slocum's left arm as Slocum made it to his feet. The others tried to dart in and grab him again, but Slocum swung wildly, driving them back. He kicked out, catching one of them square in the groin. The man folded like a paper fan.

"Christ!" Bobby Todd shouted. "Hold him!"

"He's a damn wild man!" Hoffman said.

Hoffman grabbed Slocum in a bear hug, pinning Slocum's arms to his sides, locking his face hard against the cartridges in the bandoleers.

"Stick him!" Hoffman roared.

"I can't get to his face!"

"Stick him anywheres! I can't keep holding him!"

Bobby Todd lunged forward. The bite of the iron was a searing, white-hot knife driven into the small of Slocum's back. He arched away from it, breath hissing out of his mouth.

Then a shot, and Hoffman let go and backed quickly off. Slocum turned, stumbled and went down on one

knee. Through the sweat in his eyes he saw Silas standing above Nathan, holding Slocum's pistol.

Bobby Todd whipped his own pistol out, a flurry
of blurred motion. He fired twice, so quickly the two
reports were almost one. Silas staggered, his shirt
blossoming red, the pistol dropping from his fingers.

Julia screamed.

"Goddamn it, Deward!" Bobby Todd screamed.
"You got to watch these people! That white-headed
old bastard almost punched my ticket!"

Deward seemed to swell in the saddle. He straightened, his hard gray eyes flashing and his face coloring
as if in rage. Bobby Todd, in spite of whatever anger
he might have been feeling himself, fell back a step
beneath the glare.

Deward spoke slowly, as if holding himself in. "You
don't boss to me, Bobby Todd. You don't use that kind
of talk, and never out in front of people."

Bobby Todd whirled to get away from the stare, his
own face contorted in rage. He saw Slocum, and raised
the pistol once more, thumbed back the hammer.

"Leave him," Deward said.

Bobby Todd faced his brother once more. "Leave
him hell. We didn't get it done."

"It'll do. We take the girl and go. Now. We got to use
the time we have. You know what I'm saying is true."
He gathered his reins. "Leave him and mount up."

"But I'll give him something," Bobby Todd said. He
turned and swung, bringing the pistol around, catching
Slocum across the top of the head. Slocum had ducked,
but in his pain he was slower, and the lights spewed in
bright arcs behind his eyes. He fell, landing on the iron
burn, arching his back as the ground scraped the wound
into new pain, rolling quickly over. He saw Bobby

Todd step to Nathan, place the pistol barrel against the boy's head and pull the trigger.

Conway screamed, a long, wordless howl. Slocum was on his feet in spite of the pain. Hoffman knocked him down and swung a kick at him. It missed, but the others were mounting and turning their horses, and he didn't bother to try again, but headed for his own mount. Julia had sagged against the man holding her, the one Deward had called Tyson. Her face was white, her eyes wide with disbelief. Bobby Todd grabbed her arm, and together he and Tyson shoved her up onto Bobby Todd's horse. Bobby Todd mounted after her and reached around her to grab his reins.

"Oh my God!" Conway wailed. He sank slowly to his knees. "Oh my dear God!"

As one, the riders whirled their horses and spurred back up the slope. Slocum ran to Nathan's body and grabbed the rifle. Then to the wagon, where he rested the barrel on the sideboard and fired once. He saw one of the rear riders topple from the saddle, and two others paused to return his fire, the bullets buzzing angrily past his head. They whipped their horses, hurrying up the slope behind Deward and the others. Slocum fired again, missed, and the riders topped the crest and were over.

"You did this!" Conway screamed. "You brought them here!"

He was still on his knees. His eyes blazed madly, and he pointed at Slocum, his arm rigid.

Slocum looked at him for a moment, saw the crazed terror and grief in his face, then went back to where Nathan and Silas lay. Nathan's brains were oozing out onto the dry prairie grasses, but Silas was still alive.

One of the bullet holes, high in his chest, was a sucking wound. Lung shot.

Creede was cowering behind the wagon tongue. Slocum stormed over and kicked him out into the open. "Get up, you cowardly son of a bitch!" He looked at Conway. "And you! Get off your knees! You two get that man in the wagon and hitch up the team and start lashing it into town! Now!"

"My daughter!" Conway shouted, the cords standing out on his neck.

"I'll tend to her."

Slocum laid the rifle in the bed of the wagon, went to his saddle and claimed his own Henry repeater from its scabbard. He knew this rifle, knew exactly how it shot, knew the bullets would go where he sent them. He filled his pockets with .44–40 cartridges from the box in his saddlebags.

The burn was a hot, pulsing thing on his back. Like a separate being. He moved to the nervous animals Creede had tied to the picket line. "I'm taking one of your horses, Creede," he said.

Creede offered no protest. Slocum picked a sorrel with thick hindquarters—a lot of bottom, a good mover by its looks. He mounted, whirled the horse around on a tight rein and spurred up the slope.

3

He topped the rise to the north, leaning low in the saddle in case any of them were hanging back to cover their flight. He saw them, at a dead run now, black specks thundering over the next swell, heading due west toward the mountains.

He did not allow himself to feel much yet, only the cold, deadly anger. Two men shot down and the girl taken, all in the space of twenty minutes.

And they had marked him.

They had laid a hot iron against his back and marked him. He dug the spurs in and followed at a hard, horse-killing run.

The sorrel was strong, but the animals ridden by Deward and his men were splendid, and superior. No cattleman ever raised such horses for ranch work; they were mounts made for speed and distance, for the fast getaway. But they were handicapped by Julia. Carrying double, Bobby Todd's horse would be unable to move as quickly, and as bad as they seemed to want the girl, the others would not be willing to ride ahead and leave her vulnerable.

He trailed them, waiting for the pop of rifle fire, but none of the riders turned back to brace him, though they must have known he was there. Ahead, the rolling sagebrush country gave way to the foothills, with stands of scrub pine and cedar and the occasional green swatch of willows marking the course of a creek.

Their country.

They knew it well, and Slocum knew it not at all. Soon they would be in the canyons that led into the mountains, and once they reached them, pursuit by a lone rider would not only be difficult, but foolish. There would be too many places for easy ambush, too many places where they could take him out of the saddle with one well-placed shot. If Slocum wanted to stop them, he would have to do it soon. And he would have to do it here, in the open.

He leaned farther forward in the saddle, spurring hard, yelling into the sorrel's ear. He gained on them slowly, and soon the specks became horses and men, with the girl's gray skirt billowing in the wind in front of Bobby Todd. Slocum veered more to the north, onto a flat expanse of tableland, and he gained further. He made for a stand of pine, knowing he would have one chance, and to take full advantage of it he must remain mounted.

There were perhaps a dozen wind-gnarled trees. He moved between them, close to the tallest one, and unsheathed the rifle. His hands were shaking in the aftermath of what he'd gone through, and he needed the tree to help steady him for such a foolhardy shot.

He leaned in the saddle, put his shoulder against the rough pine bark and brought the rifle up. The wound in his back bit at him, but he put it out of his mind, concentrating on the figure of Bobby Todd's running horse.

A hundred and fifty yards and the gap widening every second. Slightly downhill. No wind. It would be a crazy shot, a dangerous one. But his options were limited.

He fired. He saw Bobby Todd's horse pitch forward, both the man and the girl tumbling over its head from the saddle. In the same instant Slocum jammed spurs to the sorrel and raced toward them. He jacked another shell into the chamber. Ahead, he saw the others turn and start back to where the man and the girl were picking themselves up. Bobby Todd looked his way, and pointed. Slocum fired, worked the lever, fired again. Accuracy from a running horse was impossible, but all that mattered was to keep firing.

Come at them hard enough, fast enough, and they would scatter.

It worked. Bobby Todd ran for the nearest rider. It looked to be Tyson. Tyson slipped a foot from his stirrup, offered his hand. In a single motion Bobby Todd grabbed the hand, put his foot in the open stirrup and swung up behind, and Tyson whirled the horse and spurred away, leaving the girl there on the ground. Slocum saw the puffs of powder smoke and a split second later heard the reports of the guns, but the bullets went wide. He fired again and again, and the riders hunched over their saddles and ran. They would not go far. They would find cover and dismount and try and pick him off from the ground, but Slocum figured to be gone before they had the chance.

The girl was on her feet now, moving aimlessly, stumbling. She had one hand to her head, and Slocum hoped she was just stunned by the fall. He came to her, holding the rifle in his right hand and reaching down with his left.

"Grab my arm!"

The first bullet plowed the ground ten yards ahead of him. Another went past his head, a hornet's buzz. Julia gave no sign of having heard him. She turned and looked up the slope, toward the spot where the men had gone. Her face was still pale, stained by tears.

Cursing, Slocum sheathed the rifle and jumped down. The horse did not want to stand in the face of the bullets that were now ripping into the earth around them, and Slocum grabbed the reins high up next to the bit, at the same time catching hold of Julia's arm.

"Get up there! Up in the saddle!"

She fought him blindly, a shrill, hysterical sound coming from deep in her throat. Slocum let go of her, slapped her once, then pushed her at the horse. He got under her and shoved her up into the saddle. He mounted behind her, reached around her for the reins and kicked the horse into a run, pointing south. The bullets continued to whizz around them, and he waited for the smack of lead against flesh, or for the horse to go down, but after a few moments they had outdistanced them.

Julia's body was cold and stiff against him, and she began to shudder as she cried, her head down and both her hands gripping the saddle horn. Slocum lashed at the horse with the reins, hearing the explosive grunt of the sorrel's breath with every pound of the hooves, knowing he was killing it with hard use and the double load; but there was no choice.

He headed for the foothills, bearing south and west. If Deward and the others came after them, Slocum and the girl would need cover to survive, and the sagebrush country offered too damned little of it.

They topped a rise above a small creek, a knoll crowned by a bristling tumble of wind-weathered stone. Behind it, Slocum stopped the horse and allowed it to blow while he scouted the country for pursuit. He saw none, but still he knew it must be coming.

Their country.

He put a hand on Julia's arm. She flinched as if struck.

"You're all right now," he said, trying to make his voice soothing, reassuring. "You're all right. I've got you."

She sagged a little, and without turning reached for his arm and drew it around her, pressed herself against him as she cried. Slocum held her.

"They killed him," she said. "They just walked up and shot him—poor Nathan—"

"Yes, they did that."

"Why?"

Slocum had no answer for her. He kicked up the horse. They had to reach Garrison. Once in town they would be safe.

The cabin was a rude jumble of logs and brush with a tin chimney and a stone corral hard against the side. Three horses in the corral, fresh ones, and Slocum's mount was winded and laboring. The sun had gone down behind the peaks, and the wind that whipped at them had an icy edge to it.

Smoke came from the chimney in a steady stream. Slocum smelled food cooking.

Two and a half, maybe three hours since their flight from the tablelands, and no sign of Deward or the others. Still, Slocum's natural caution, his alertness, was very much alive, in spite of the fiery, throbbing ache of the running-iron burn. He didn't know how far from the town of Garrison they might be—perhaps they had even gone past it by now—but he knew they needed a fresh horse or they would not make it.

They were well into the foothills now, the ragged, pine-studded and rocky canyons. He studied the cabin from a stand of cedar a hundred yards away. There was a clearing, but the ground was uneven and the soil thin, and there was no crop and no place to put one. Not a farmer. A prospector, maybe.

He looked up at Julia, who teetered wearily in the saddle. "You wait here. Hang on a little longer, can you do that?"

She nodded slowly, as if too tired to even speak.

"You see anything, hear any noise in the brush, anything that might be those men coming back, you scream out. I'll come running. All right?"

Another nod. She looked at him, her eyes soft and vulnerable. "I'll be fine," she said, her voice barely above a whisper. "Thank you."

Slocum hesitated, not wanting to leave her here alone, and at the same time unwilling to take her down to the cabin until he knew it was safe.

Finally he left her there and walked into the clearing. He approached the cabin slowly, the Henry rifle held loosely in his right hand, careful to make no movements that could be mistaken for hostile. At forty yards he stopped and called, "Hello the cabin!"

A thin, bent man appeared at the door. He was unarmed, dressed in black pants and a smudged and faded red vest. He was bearded like an Old Testament prophet.

"What do you want coming around my house? You hurt?"

Slocum stood where he was and explained their need for a fresh horse and their willingness to trade. "I've got a woman with me, and I need to fetch her to town before night. Be obliged to you."

The man ruminated on it for a moment. His chin moved up, then down, carrying the rat's nest beard with it. "All right," he said at last. "Bring your animal down here and we'll have look at what you got."

"You alone here?"

"All by myself."

"You got any objections if I was to take a look for myself?"

The man stiffened, as if insulted, but he stood aside as Slocum came forward to peer past the door of the little cabin. A tangled bachelor's quarters smelling of smoke and old clothing.

The man's jaw dropped when Slocum brought Julia into the dooryard. He stood as if spiked to the ground, his red-veined eyes wide in their sockets. Slocum suspected the sight of any woman could have produced the same reaction in the man.

Slocum helped Julia down. The man stepped forward and introduced himself as Lester Fields, and grinned to reveal teeth that were both bad and few, though he was not much past fifty. Julia nodded wearily and smiled. The sorrel stood with its head low, and Fields took a walk around it, inspecting it; but his eyes kept moving to Julia, then flicking to Slocum.

"I'll let you have one of my nags," Fields said. "Go ahead and strip the saddle off this one and turn him out in that pen yonder. Y'all look like you could use some provender. I got some supper left. Come on in, Missy, and I'll fix you a plate."

"She'll stay with me," Slocum said. "We'll come in together."

Fields's lips thinned beneath the beard, but he said nothing as Slocum stripped the rigging from the sorrel and led it into the little stone corral. Slocum gave Julia the rifle to hold and kept himself between her and Fields. He had expected Fields to return to the cabin, but the man hovered there, waiting, making Slocum uneasy. When they were finished, the three of them walked to the cabin together.

"Ain't much, but you're welcome to it," Fields said, ushering them inside. "Find you a place to sit, knock that junk off them chairs, don't pay no mind to it."

Slocum brushed pieces of old harness from a chair and offered it to Julia. He had the rifle and chose to remain standing; he watched as Fields found two tin plates and wiped them off with a rag. There was a spindly-legged table in the center of the cabin, and Fields laid a couple of plates on it. An old Army Colt lay there close to the edge, oiled and loaded.

The room was cramped and cluttered with two old saddles, a shovel and two picks, an old gold rocker and piles of unidentifiable litter; but it was warm from the cook fire. A covered Dutch oven hung on an iron frame over the fireplace.

"Town's ten miles southeast," Fields said. "Get dark quick. I think you ought to stay here the night."

"No thanks," Slocum said.

"The girl can have the bed in here, me and you can bunk outside. Got an extra bedroll for you."

"No," Slocum said.

Fields moved to the fire, lifted the lid of the Dutch oven with a rag and stirred the contents. He straightened, looked at Slocum, then glanced again at Julia. His eyes could not seem to stay in one place.

"You look pretty bunged up. Somebody jump you?"

"Had some hard times," Slocum said. "I'll get over it."

"You really oughtn't to travel, wore out as the both of you look. You stay over you can have some liniment for your aches, doctor yourself up. Better if you do. Matter of fact, I insist on it."

Slocum said, "Julia, go outside and wait for me."

She looked up at him questioningly.

"Do it now," Slocum said. "Go."

She rose and hurried out. Fields scowled at him from beside the fire.

"Mister, you don't seem to hear very well," Slocum said. "I thank you for the offer of hospitality, but I believe we'll be riding on."

"You ain't going nowhere," Fields snarled. He tilted forward and his right arm whipped behind him. Slocum dove to the right as the knife flashed past him to stick, blade thrumming, in the back wall. He brought the rifle up as Fields lunged for the pistol on the table. He fired once, the gunshot savagely loud in the tiny room, and Fields was smashed back against the wall beside the fireplace. Fields stood there a moment, nervous eyes still flicking, his hands clasped high up on his belly where blood began to trickle from between his fingers. Then he sagged and slid to the dirt floor.

His mouth worked. Slocum stepped closer to him, the rifle at the ready.

"Joshua," Fields said. "For old Joshua."

In a moment he was dead. Slocum left him there and went outside. Julia stood stiff in the dooryard under a darkening sky and looked at him.

"You killed him," she said, her voice strangely flat.

"He forced it."

She nodded once. "What—" she said. Faltered. "What did he want?"

"Seemed like he wanted you, ma'am. If you'll step over there by the corral you won't have to see him when I bring him out."

She shook her head, choosing to remain where she was. Slocum went back inside and dragged the dead man out. He took him back of the cabin among the trees and brush and left him there. He should bury him, he thought, but he possessed neither the energy nor the pity the job required.

When he returned, Julia said, "Are we leaving now?"

"There's food in there. We'd best eat while we can."

The Dutch oven held beans and meat. They ate, Julia at the table and Slocum standing in the center of the room. They had lighted a single lamp. The food was tasteless, but filling.

"Those men who came," she said. "Had you seen them before?"

"No."

"Why? Why did they do what they did to you?"

Slocum told her about his encounter with Rory Halsey last night in the town of Garrison. He told her also of similar folk he had known back home in Georgia, before the war, clannish mountain people who rallied around each other at first sign of trouble. Whip one, you had to whip them all.

She said, "I haven't thanked you yet for coming after me."

"I did what had to be done."

"Is it that simple? Whatever has to be done, you do?"

"I felt responsible. If it hadn't been for me, they wouldn't have come. Your cousin would still be alive."

She nodded and lowered her head. Then she said, "Why don't you sit down? You must be as exhausted as I am. Probably more."

Slocum pulled the other chair from the table and sat down, wincing as the burn scraped the back of the chair and caught fire again.

"Wait," she said. "Let me have a look at that."

Slocum shook his head, but she insisted. He rose and pulled up his shirt, and she bent to inspect the wound.

"It looks angry," she said. "Let me find a rag that's halfway clean and I'll wash it, and put on a dressing."

"I'll be fine until we get to town."

"Hush. Men never know what's good for them."

She brought a bucket of fresh water from the barrel outside the front door. There was a bed in the corner of the cabin, a bunk of raw timber with a straw mattress, and she stripped it of its filthy blankets. She made Slocum remove his shirt and lie down, and she knelt over him with the water. No clean rags were to be found, so she tore a piece from her skirt.

Slocum sucked in a sharp breath as she began dabbing at the wound. "Try to rest easy," she said. "It'll be over in a moment."

Slocum felt himself stir as she tended to him. She rested her free hand on his back as she washed him with the other, and her skin was cool and smooth against his own. When she was finished she found a mound of butter in waxed paper and smeared it over the burn. Slocum rolled over and looked at her.

There was longing in her face, and confusion and sorrow. She ran her hand up through the hair on his chest, then bent and kissed him softly on the lips.

Slocum returned the kiss, gently at first and then with more heat, his fingers weaving into her hair. Her lips parted and their tongues touched.

She broke the kiss and placed her head on his chest. "Oh God. Hold me, please, John."

He pulled her down onto the bed beside him and cradled her in his arms. She arched into him, against him. He kept waiting for her to cry again, but she did not. After long minutes she took his hand and placed it on her breast. He felt the nipple under his palm, beneath the fabric, and as he stroked it, she opened her lips for a deeper kiss.

All the tension of the last six hours welled up in them, and they ground at each other, in search of release. He reached under her skirt to cup the rounded swell of her buttocks, and she surged against his leg, her own hand coming up to rip at the buttons of her bodice. In moments her breasts were free. They were round and full, their skin so taut that they seemed to gleam in the lamplight. Slocum covered one small pink nipple with his mouth, brushed it with his tongue. She cupped his head and pulled him more firmly against her softness, gasping.

Slocum was lashed by sudden, delicious waves of desire. Her lips were open, yielding, her breath hot and moist. Her body asked him for no gentleness now. No time for long, languid moves. Her hands on his back pulled at him. Fingernails dug in. She lifted herself as he pulled at her undergarments, helping him. His fingers traveled across the soft mound and found the center of her warmth, dipped deep within and felt it hot and slick and beckoning to him. She fumbled at his belt and his buttons, freed him, grasped the engorged shaft. He pulsed against her hand.

She guided him in. She was wet and ready and demanded all of him. He plunged the full length, and she arched into it, her head snapping back, mouth falling open in a silent cry. And again and once more, and each time she met him halfway, their two bodies slamming together in the air.

She clasped herself to him, and with each thrust she gave tiny cries that increased in volume and length until at last they became one continuous and high-pitched moan and her hips were rolling. She shuddered around him. Slocum swelled inside her and the spasm began, irrevocable and thunderous, a great fiery wave that was quivering and endless. She cried out again and seemed to peak higher as she felt him course into her.

Afterward, drained, they lay quietly together, still joined, and allowed their heartbeats to slow to normal. Her arms were around his neck. Finally, she broke down and cried again softly. Slocum held her.

4

They set out before daylight the next morning, Slocum riding the sorrel and Julia mounted on one of the horses from the stone corral, astride with her skirt bunched up around the saddle. Her bare legs were pale in the crisp morning air.

Fields had lied to them. Garrison lay less than five miles to the southeast, and they arrived as the sun broke above the sage lands.

Mr. Conway rushed out from the Garrison House Hotel as they came up the street. His clothes were rumpled and stained, his face lined and drawn with lack of sleep. He kept saying, "Thank God, Julia, oh, thank God," over and over.

He helped his daughter down and hugged her. Slocum dismounted and Conway came over and thrust out his pudgy hand. "I thank you, sir. That's all I can say, and it's poor expression for what I feel. She's all I've got left now."

Slocum shook the hand. "Silas?"

Conway lowered his head. He tried to speak, stammered, then started again. "He didn't make it. Passed away in the wagon."

Slocum cursed lowly.

"I left Nathan at the—" Conway halted, took a breath. "I left him at the undertakers here. Mr. Creede's heading back to Denver. He's offered to transport him to the train for us."

"You see the Marshal?"

Conway's face darkened. "I saw him. He wasn't much help."

"Doesn't surprise me. Is there a doctor here?"

"I found one. Of course, the wound on your back. You'll need him to see to it."

"Your daughter already took care of that. I want to ask him about something else. But first I'm going to see Marshal Reed."

Conway had booked rooms in the Garrison House. He offered to book one for Slocum as well, so that he might get cleaned up and rest. Slocum thanked him. "I'll be along directly," he said. Julia took his hand and squeezed it, and mouthed the words *thank you* as her father led her away.

The door to the Marshal's office was locked, the windows dark. On the sidewalk outside Slocum stopped a starched store clerk on his way to work and asked him if the Marshal slept here or had a place somewhere else. The clerk, looking startled, told him Reed was probably inside. The man wasn't often seen on the street before eleven o'clock or so.

"Does most of his patrolling at night," the clerk explained.

"I know what he does at night," Slocum said. He released the man, who promptly scurried away. Slocum raised a boot and kicked the door open.

Reed's private room was in the back, to the right of the cells behind the office. Reed was on his feet in his union suit, fumbling at the scarred top of an old dresser for his pistols. His long hair was tangled, and his eyes were bleary. Slocum lanced forward, like the strike of a snake, and twisted the pistol away from him.

Reed snatched for the second gun. Slocum spun the pistol, cocked it. "Leave it," he said.

Reed dropped his hand and stepped away. He stared at Slocum, fully awake now, his face burning with resentment.

"You need to sleep lighter," Slocum said. "Or lean a little less on the whiskey."

"I could arrest you for breaking in here," Reed said.

Slocum hefted the pistol experimentally. "You could try."

Reed continued to burn, arms held rigid at his sides, his back board-straight. "You got a speech for me, go ahead and spit it out."

"There's two men dead, and a woman almost kidnapped. You plan on doing anything about it?"

"You mean the little set-to that city man told me about yesterday." His lips twitched into the hint of a smirk. "Deward found you. I figured he might. You brought it down on yourself, mister."

"Nobody brings a thing like that down on himself, not alone. It's pushed on him."

"You pushed back, did you?"

"Best I could at the time. And I ain't done pushing yet."

Reed, still smirking, said, "Happened well outside of town. You want the sheriff, not me. He's up in Denver. My jurisdiction ends down the street there where them buildings quit."

"Maybe you could get off your dead ass and wire him."

Reed cocked his head back. His eyes narrowed. "Already did."

"And I suppose he's helling it down here."

"I dunno. I ain't heard yet."

"Where's the Halseys' home range? Or do they light in the trees like buzzards?"

"What they done to you wasn't enough," Reed said. "You want to go looking for more. My advice to you is leave those people the hell alone. They will kill you next time, and not think twice. Or somebody else will."

"Meaning?"

"Meaning they got a lot of friends around here. You go stirring up trouble with them, you're likely to find you got more enemies than anything else."

"I got one less enemy now. There's a man named Fields, had a cabin about five miles northwest, up in the foothills. Who was he?"

"Was?"

"He's dead. Come at me with a knife."

"You spread brightness and sunshine wherever you go, don't you, Slocum? It wasn't his cabin. Fields worked for old Joshua Halsey as a hired hand. Been with him for years. That was a line shack on the Halseys' property. Those boys ain't going to be much happier about that than they were about Rory getting shot."

"How do you feel about it, Marshal?"

Reed shifted his weight from one foot to the other. He crossed his arms over his chest. "I told you, I'm City Marshal, nothing else. You bring it into town and I'll have to deal with it. Otherwise it ain't my business."

"Somehow I have a hard time swallowing that."

"If you're smart you'll ride north and not slow down until you reach Idaho. I ain't answering any more questions. Either shoot me or get the hell out of my room."

Slocum tossed the pistol onto the dresser with its mate. It landed with a heavy thump and scarred the wood, leaving a raw pale mark against what was left of the darker finish. "You'll be seeing me again," he said.

"No doubt," Reed said. "The question is whether you'll be standing up, or laid out with pennies over your eyes."

After leaving Reed's office, Slocum headed for the telegraph station. The clerk there was surly and uncooperative, and when Slocum asked if any wires had been sent to the sheriff up in Denver the past two days, he refused to answer, saying that such information was privileged and not to be given out to the general dirty-necked population. Slocum dragged the man halfway across the counter by his collar and repeated the question.

The clerk went through his papers. No such telegram had been sent.

Slocum asked a few more questions. Dr. Reddick's place, he was told, was up the street, last house on the right at the edge of town. Slocum headed in that direction.

He sensed that Marshal Lacklin Reed could prove troublesome. In spite of the man's claim of impartiality, if he wasn't smack in the middle of the Halseys' camp, he was at least sympathetic to it. Deward had known Slocum's name, and had known which direction he'd ridden. While Deward could have learned these things almost anywhere on the street, Slocum had a gut feeling that the information had come from Reed and nobody else.

Dr. Reddick's place was a simple plank house, one of the few in town painted white. There was a fenced yard out front and a gravel drive on which patients could park their buggies.

Dr. Reddick himself was a small but sturdy man in his mid-forties, with brown hair that was almost red and a trim mustache. He made Slocum remove his shirt so that he could examine the burn on his back. He cleaned it again and applied a cooling salve. He swabbed iodine on the cuts and abrasions on Slocum's face.

"They never brought Rory here," he said. "And they never called for me to go up there to tend it for him. They wouldn't have done it if you'd shot his arm completely off. They keep to themselves, those people."

"He'll have to have something done about it," Slocum said.

"It'll go to rot, likely, or kill him of blood poisoning. They don't have the sense God gave a goose, and there's a whole nest of them up in those hills. You're a Southerner yourself, I can tell by your voice. I mean you no disrespect personally, but that bunch is the vilest trash ever to come out of the Confederacy. Supposed to have ridden with Quantrill or Bloody Bill Anderson, so they say. They settled here after the war, running from the carpetbaggers. Pretty quick they brought in every uncle and cousin and shirttail relative they had."

"You know them well?"

"I know where their place is up there, if that's what you're asking."

"It is."

"The folks around here are well acquainted with the Halseys. The old man, Joshua, cut a wide swath for quite a while. Haven't seen or heard of him in some time. His son Deward's pretty much taken over the mantle, but I imagine old Joshua still runs him when he's of a mind."

Slocum recalled Fields's dying words—*Joshua. For old Joshua.*

He said, "What is it they do up there?"

"Run cattle, a few horses. Or that's what they'll tell you if you come asking. But if there's a stage robbery within fifty miles, or a bank job in Denver or Colorado Springs, or a dead man found in a gully with his pockets turned out, you can figure they probably had a hand in it. If you're going up after them, you be careful. They swarm like bees. They'll pick the flesh off your bones."

"Can you tell me where I'll find them?"

"You could get that information almost anywhere in town."

"Any reason I can't get it from you?"

Reddick considered it. "No, I don't suppose there is."

He went to the big rolltop desk in the corner of the examining room and began scratching out a map on a clean sheet of paper. Slocum put his shirt back on, listening to the scrape of the pen. When Reddick finished, he handed the map to Slocum.

"Obliged," Slocum said. He folded the map into a square and tucked it in his pocket.

"There's a woman up there acts as a doctor for them," Reddick said. "An old crone, I forget her name. If Rory Halsey wants attention given to that arm he'll likely go to her. She's no better than a damned Indian medicine man, or a witch doctor, throwing herbs and berries around."

"You know where her place is?"

"No. She could live in a burrow with coyotes for all I know." Reddick regarded him thoughtfully. "You're a hard-looking man, Slocum. There's a lot of scars on you, and the tracks of other doctors before me. You get that chewed up in the War?"

"And various other places."

"The burn I just treated. The Halseys put that on you?"

"They did."

"Then God help them. And you."

5

Mr. Conway had rented a room for Slocum on the second floor of the Garrison House. Conway's own room was next door, and Julia's one down from that. The father had placed himself between Slocum and his daughter. The fact made Slocum smile. The memory of Julia's body beneath his own was still fresh, and he wondered if Conway had sensed something, the way fathers sometimes did.

His Colt Navy was on the bed, carried back by Conway, with dust still on the oiled barrel and cylinder. His saddlebags lay beside it. Slocum checked to see that his money was still there. It was. A note on the dresser invited him to join father and daughter for supper at six o'clock.

He washed at the basin and shaved, and climbed between clean sheets. When he woke it was nearing dusk and he felt refreshed. He dressed and went down to the lobby, where he found Julia and Mr. Conway waiting for him.

Julia wore a fresh dress. Conway had apparently found time to toss their baggage on the wagon before

49

bringing Silas into town, and Slocum felt a pinch of irritation, wondering if such a delay could have contributed to the old man's death.

When Julia saw Slocum, she smiled, and then tried to hide it from her father by looking down at the toes of her shoes. Conway was in a pair of black, expensive-looking trousers and a gray suit coat. He had found a black band somewhere and wore it upon his arm to announce the mourning of his dead nephew. His cheeks were pink from the razor, and his face still just as full and round, but somehow he looked drawn, as if the last twenty-four hours had taken a heavy toll.

"Mr. Slocum," he said. "You've accepted our invitation, then?"

The thought of spending the evening across a table from the man whose daughter he had just bedded was distasteful to Slocum. He said, "I'll sit with you a few minutes."

The dining room was nearly empty at this hour. It had polished hardwood floors and shining brass chandeliers and a ceiling of pressed tin. They sat at a table near the big draped windows, and Conway ordered coffee. It was brought. Slocum set his menu aside without looking at it.

"I must apologize to you," Conway said. "My words yesterday afternoon were harsh and uncalled for. It was the strain of the moment and I hope you can overlook it."

"Understood."

"Julia told me of your ordeal getting back to town last night. Again I offer you my thanks."

At the mention of last night Slocum felt Julia's foot brush his leg. He glanced at her. She was looking at her father, innocent and passive.

Conway went on, "I'm sending Julia back to Chicago with Nathan's—with Nathan. I'll remain here a short time."

Julia said, "Dad, I told you, if you're staying, I'm staying."

"Hush," Conway said. "Slocum, I want those men. I want them for what they did to Nathan, and what they tried to do to my daughter. I want you to get them for me. I can pay you. A great deal of money."

Conway sat back in his chair and waited.

There it was, Slocum thought. And then he thought, *shit*. The last thing he needed was some little potbellied city man prodding at him.

"Mr. Conway," he said, "what you need to do is take your daughter and your dead nephew and hop a train for Chicago just as fast as you can."

Conway shook his head. "I won't even think about it."

"Then you're not thinking at all. I managed to get your daughter back from them yesterday. But they didn't just take her because she was pretty, I'm sure of that. They had plans for her. The man who fought me in that cabin yesterday fought me because of her. If they come after her again I may not be around to stop them."

"They wouldn't dare come after her here," Conway said.

"This is their country. It might be their town. The City Marshal doesn't strike me as sympathetic."

"Damn it, Slocum," Conway said. "I've got to take that boy's body back to Chicago and face my sister and tell her how he died. I won't tell her that I ran away from it."

"Go home, Mr. Conway."

"Look at what they did to you! They burned you, man. Don't you want to make them pay?"

Slocum bored into Conway with his eyes, and at last the plump man's gaze fell. Slocum said, "They marked me, Mr. Conway, that's true. There'll be a reckoning for it. But nobody buys me, no matter what the reason. When the reckoning comes, I don't want to have to be worried about two other people."

He rose from the table and put his hat back on. He touched the brim politely. "Enjoy your suppers." He turned and strode out into the deepening dusk.

He ate at a chop stand in a saloon at the lower end of town. He washed the meal down with two whiskeys. The bartender was a thick man with a graying beard. Slocum engaged him in seemingly innocent conversation, the whole time lacing his words with mention of the Halseys, hoping the man would open up.

Just when he'd decided to try his luck in a different saloon, he saw one of them.

This bar catered to the rougher element, which was exactly the reason Slocum had chosen it. He saw his man in the corner closest to the front door, bent over a table, talking earnestly to someone.

One of those who'd been with Deward yesterday, a minor player. Fairly young, with a shock of blond hair hanging out beneath the uptilted brim of his shapeless hat. A bony face. Slocum remembered the man at his right leg, helping to hold him down while Bobby Todd brought out the hot running iron.

He hadn't seen Slocum. Slocum stepped farther back into the corner, rolled and lighted a cigarette, tugged his hat low over his face and watched.

The blond man gestured with his arm toward the street, then straightened, still looking at his friend, as if waiting. His friend nodded and rose. Slocum didn't know this one. A little shorter than the blond man, dark hair and large ears. Together they headed for the batwing doors, determination in their steps. They pushed through them and outside. Slocum waited a few seconds, then drained the last of his drink and followed.

He would see what they were up to before calling them out. Maybe they'd lead him to some of the others.

It was full dark now, the street illuminated by the lamps of the various drinking houses. He saw the blond man step to a horse at the hitch rail and pull a gun from the saddle sheath. Shotgun, it looked like, twin barrels. He tucked it into the crook of his arm, and the two men continued up the street, past the saloons and cathouses toward the intersection with Main Street. They walked close together, heads tilted in, talking lowly. Slocum tossed his cigarette away and trailed them at a discreet distance.

At Main they turned left, into the respectable section of town.

Toward the hotel.

They spread out a little now, as if the words were all done with and just the job, whatever it was, remained. They kept to the street, off the boardwalks, as if wanting to make as little noise as possible. At a corner across and down from the hotel they paused, and then the shorter, dark-haired man angled off as if to approach the hotel from around the stables on the opposite side of the street. The blond man began walking, shotgun still cradled, toward the hotel's front porch.

Mr. Conway came around the corner, a lighted cigar between his knuckles.

"Mr. Slocum!" he called. "A few words with you, please!"

He heard the blond man say, "*Slocum!*" Saw him whirl. The shotgun came up. Slocum jumped to the left as the gun blast ripped at the darkness. He felt the buckshot cut through the air close to him, and as he hit the ground, he rolled, coming out of it with the Navy Colt in his fist, ready for the second blast to erupt.

But the blond man had run, and his partner was following, back down Main toward the rougher section. Slocum got up and holstered the pistol, not wishing to waste powder and shot.

Conway had plastered himself against the locked doorway of a dark storefront, his eyes wide and the cigar on the boardwalk at his feet. Slocum stood in front of him, hands on hips.

"I told you they'd be back," he said. "They were headed for the hotel. For your daughter."

Conway blinked at him, still pressed against the door.

"Go home, Mr. Conway."

6

Early the next morning Slocum rode into the foothills.

Up above the sage and scrub oak, into the spruce and yellow pine and slick rock, he found the trail indicated by Reddick's map. In some places it was no bigger than a snake track through the brush. Six or seven miles and he began to see cabins scattered here and there among the trees. He avoided them. He left the trail where he could and cut across country, watching always for sentries but seeing none, heading to the northwest and the spot on the map that should be the Halseys' home place.

An hour later he found it. He came onto it from the high side, and at the top of a wooded rise he looked down past a stand of aspen and studied the house, the outbuildings and corrals, and the chickens scratching around in the yard.

It was a larger place than the others he'd passed, with a porch and a long, low roof of tar paper. A small pole barn and corral sat off to the side. It lay in a steep canyon, hard against the slope, with a creek hissing down through the corrals for water. A mule and a dirty white horse stood, swishing tails at flies.

Nothing else. No other horses, no sign of Deward or any of the rest, no indication they'd ever been here.

He heard a door slam, and a blond girl emerged from the house, carrying a bowl of something into the sun-washed dirt and pine needles of the yard. A small girl—woman, he corrected, seeing the swell of hip and breast. Her bare feet splashed dust.

She went around the pole barn and dumped the contents of the bowl—slops—into a hog pen, banged it against one of the fence posts to clean it of last dregs, then stood and watched the hogs quarrel and fuss over the food. One naked foot was bent back, toe tracing idly in the dirt. Then she turned and headed for the house, shooing chickens out of the way.

Slocum rode down into the yard and stopped ten feet from the edge of the house. She halted, holding the bowl before her with both hands, staring at him.

"You the law?" she asked.

He shook his head. "Where are they?"

"I don't know. Ain't been here in two days. I don't care if they never show up again."

She looked as if she meant it, head back at an angry cant, eyes flashing—eyes that even from where he was, fifteen feet away, Slocum could see were blue. Her breasts were thrust proudly forward, and he could tell that she wore nothing beneath the dress. Her nipples poked out at him through the fabric.

"Mind if I look around?"

"What'd they do to you?"

"Enough."

"They kill anybody this time?"

Slocum nodded. She looked at him a few moments more. He could see her nostrils flaring as she breathed. At last she said, "You can look around if you want, but not in the house. My daddy's in there, and he's ailing."

"That would be Joshua."

She blinked, surprised. "How'd you know that?"

"I'd like to talk to him a minute."

"You can't. He's bad sick. He can't do for himself no more at all. He can't get out of bed or feed himself or even go to the privvy. They run off and left me here to care for him by myself."

"They are your brothers?"

She nodded once, the bowl still in front of her, as if she might raise it and use it for a shield. "What's your name, mister?"

"John Slocum."

"You best leave them be, John Slocum. They're bad. They done something to you, and they killed somebody, you say. Well, they done it before. Lots of times. They won't hold from killing you, either, you mess with them any more. If my daddy could get out of bed, and if he knew you'd come after them, he'd kill you."

"Was your daddy as bad as Deward and Bobby Todd?"

"He was worse."

"I want to talk to him."

"Won't do you no good," she said, but her defiance was not as strong. The words came out almost a sigh.

Slocum dismounted and tied his horse to the porch. She walked to the door, head down, bowl banging against her knees. The dress was tight and sleek against the swell of her hips, showing the graceful, taut curve of her buttocks. Twenty, maybe, Slocum thought. Perhaps younger. She went inside, leaving the door open for Slocum to follow her, or not, as he chose.

The interior of the cabin was spartan, neat, with a dirt floor carefully swept. An old cookstove still pulsed heat, and the air held the fragrance of food recently cooked. Underneath these smells was the sour, fetid odor of sickness. A curtain hung from the bare rafters, sectioning off sleeping quarters.

The girl went to the table that stood in the center of the big room and placed the bowl on it. She sat down, her back to Slocum. She did not look around.

"In there," she said. She made a terse gesture toward the curtain.

Slocum pulled the curtain back. An iron bedstead, heaped with comforters. The sour smell was thicker here, almost overpowering—body fluids, waste, the sweat of illness. The man in the bed watched him with one eye. The other was canted off to the left, open, staring, glazed.

Not an ancient man. Mature, in his sixties, but his skin was waxy, yellowish, and slack and loose as if the man inside it had dwindled. Moisture from his mouth had seeped out onto his chin. The left side of his face was twisted, giving him a permanent snarl. She had just shaved him. There was still blood on his cheek from a razor nick.

Slocum did not bother to ask the questions he wanted answered. The old man had suffered some sort of stroke, and looked done for. The comforters barely moved with his breathing.

"I told you it wouldn't do you no good," the girl said. She had come up behind Slocum and stood there holding the curtain aside, looking at her father.

"How long's he been this way?" Slocum asked.

"I don't know, a month maybe. Six weeks. He just keeled over one day and couldn't get back up."

"You had a doctor see to him?"

"The old woman's looked at him," she said, and then clamped her lips shut and glanced away.

"That would be the old doctor woman I've heard lives up here. Where's her place?"

"She won't talk to you, either."

"Where?"

She pointed. "Half a mile that way. She's got the house painted white, onliest painted house anywhere around here. What do you want to see her for?"

Slocum chose not to answer that. "What's your name?"

"Lorine. And you're John Slocum. There ain't nobody on this mountain going to help you find my brothers, John Slocum. Everybody's close, everybody's kin, even that old woman. Anybody finds out what you're after, they'll grab a gun and shoot you. Every last one of them will."

"I don't see you grabbing for a gun."

"That's because I'm different."

That she was. Young and healthy and sunburned, looking at him with a steady, calm gaze. In a town girl it would be called bold. The front of her dress was unbuttoned two buttons down, showing the freckles on her skin just below the hollow of her throat. The skin would be warm there, and smooth, and taste faintly of salt.

She said, "You better go now."

Slocum nodded. He looked at old Joshua one last time. The old man lay there barely breathing, staring back at him with his one good eye.

She followed him out to his horse. He swung up into the saddle.

"I'd ask you to come back," she said, "but if I did it would be stupid. They found you here you wouldn't have a chance."

"And you don't know where they are."

She shook her head.

"If you asked me to come back, brothers or no brothers, I'd come."

He reined his horse around, heading it in the direction she'd indicated, toward the old woman's place. He glanced behind him once and saw her still in the yard, staring after him.

Through the trees, red fir and aspen, the snake-track road wider now, showing places where wagons and horses had passed with some regularity, and then breaking out into a clearing, a marshy meadow. Maybe a quarter mile along and no more cabins for a while.

Slocum reined up before entering the clearing and scanned the edge of the trees all around, and the base of the rocky scarp to the right and the tumble of granite above. It would be a bad spot in which to make a mistake, in the open with no cover.

At the far end a rider emerged from the trees.

A dirty brown shirt, shapeless gray hat and the thin beard below it, but most prominent from this distance, about a hundred yards, was the bundle laid across the pommel of the saddle in front of him, something wrapped up as if in a white sheet. Slocum waited, and saw that the rider was one of the younger brothers, the one Deward had called Tyson, and that he was unaware Slocum was there, watching him. Slocum allowed him to get within thirty yards, then walked his horse out of the woods to meet him.

"Hey," he called, easily.

Tyson reined up. Blinked. A flash of panic whipped across his face and was gone in an instant, replaced by grim anger.

"You're in the wrong place, mister," he said.

"I'd like to have a word with your brothers. You left so quick the other day I didn't have the chance to finish our little talk."

"What brothers? Maybe I don't know who you're talking about."

"Deward and Bobby Todd."

"I don't figger they'll want to hear anything you got to say."

"Let them tell me that. Where are they?"

Tyson watched him, his eyes moving, and Slocum could tell he was gauging the distance between them, trying to decide how and when to make his move and what his chances were. The grips of his pistol stuck up from his belt, and there was a rifle in the saddle scabbard at his knee.

"Don't you try it," Slocum told him.

Tyson's eyebrows cinched down, his face showing angry defiance. "Tell me what to try, son of a—"

He spurred his horse as he drew, the last words of his oath cut off by the flurry of movement. Slocum saw the pistol coming up, snagging on the belt. Tyson jerked at it, mouth open and snarling, and Slocum whipped the Navy Colt from its holster and fired.

Twenty feet. The bullet took Tyson square in the center of the chest and hurled him over and off the horse. The horse spooked at the shot and trampled him getting away; Slocum heard the thud and the grunt as the hooves struck the man's body. The horse ran across the clearing, slowed, then stopped to turn back and stand, looking toward

Slocum dejectedly, as if ashamed of itself for the display.

Tyson lay kicking in the marshy grass, his pistol on the ground out of his reach. His face had gone gray pale, and the blood pumped from the chest wound in time with the beating of his heart.

"Oh, Jesus Christ," he wailed. "Oh shit!"

Slocum dismounted and walked to him. The white bundle Tyson had carried was on the ground, stained with mud and moisture. Slocum picked it up and unwrapped it, and just as quickly dropped it again.

It was a severed human arm.

"You leave that be!" Tyson cried. "That's Rory's. You shot it off, you son of a bitch, now you leave it be!" He turned as the pain seized him, and pressed his face into the ground. His hands gripped at the wound as if to stop the flow of blood. They were bright red to the wrists. "Oh, God, mister, I don't want to die."

"You're going to, boy. You might redeem yourself from such a misspent youth if you was to tell me what I need to know."

"That arm's Rory's," he said again. "It was going bad on him, was fixing to poison him, so the old woman sawed it off, us holding him down and him screaming like a girl. She knows what to do about those things. Take me there, mister, she'll fix me—"

There was an edge of hysteria in his voice, almost a laugh. Quavering and high-pitched.

"Where are they, boy?"

"We left it with her. She was going to feed it to her hogs. The arm. Then Deward says to me I got to go and get it. Deward wants it buried on home ground."

Rambling. Losing hold on being here. Slocum pressed him.

"You're dying. Tell me where they are."

"I'll tell you. Because you'll go there, and they'll kill you for this. They'll blast your ass clean to hell. I'll see you there before breakfast and we'll sizzle and pop together. Cousin's ranch, about two miles up there, north. Go on. Go there, and die."

7

He left Tyson's body in the brush and, carrying the bundled arm with him, left the trail and inched his way across country, through aspen and spruce and tumbled, broken rock. He took his bearings at the crest of each ridge, angling ever northward.

Two miles. The ranch of some cousin. How many cousins could they have, these people? How many of them were there?

Go there, and die.

He came on the ranch from above, working his way around a granite shelf that tilted out from the shoulder of the mountainside. He left his horse behind, crept out on the shelf and squatted next to a tumble of wind-scarred boulders. He studied the place.

A cluster of squat, rough-hewn log buildings, dominated by a leaning barn. They were settled in a broad little canyon that was watered by twin creeks. The lodgepole corrals were filled with at least a dozen drowsing horses.

Men in the yard. Two of them came from the barn, heading for one of the low buildings that must serve as the main house. Carrying rifles. Another moved toward a stand of pine, holding something in his arms. His size was obvious even from Slocum's position, two hundred yards up the mountain—the red-haired man, the one they'd called Hoffman. Under the pines they had set up a bed, and a man lay in it, covered by a dark blanket.

I've got your arm up here, Rory, Slocum thought.

The thing Hoffman was carrying turned out to be a tray of food, and it looked as if he were trying to get Rory to eat something. Slocum saw Deward come from the house, and saw several others he recognized by their clothes, as well as a woman in a shapeless dress and some bare-legged children playing in the dirt. No Bobby Todd.

It wasn't a good place to try and take them. He might open up from here with the rifle, but he could only score a few hits before the rest of them reached cover. And it wouldn't be as good that way.

Wait, then. Catch them out alone, or in small groups. He didn't want all of them, only the ones who had been at the camp, the ones who had marked him, or had sat still and allowed it to happen.

Not today. But he could send them a message. He stepped out from the boulders.

It didn't take long. After a minute or so, someone spotted him and pointed. He heard small splashes of talk and saw them scurry around, like ants. The sun was high overhead. Deward squinted up at him, one hand shading his face. Hoffman came over, and he and Deward exchanged a few words—heated words by the looks of it—after which Hoffman headed for the barn. He returned a few minutes later leading a saddled horse, then mounted up and spurred the animal out onto the brown strip of trail that led around the base of the mountain.

Just the one man. Apparently they figured it was all they needed. Slocum smiled. He moved back to his own horse.

He went quickly down the far side of the hill. At the base of the ridge the lodgepoles grew in a thick stand, a few young ones among them struggling to survive. Slocum unlashed the lariat from his saddle and, standing precariously upon the back of his horse, looped the rope around one of the short high branches and tied it fast to the trunk.

In a few minutes he was done. He led his horse back among the trees, where it would be less likely to catch a stray bullet.

He heard Hoffman coming, angling down off the trail, the shod hooves of his animal cracking against the shattered rock. He leaned against a tree and waited, his rifle cocked and ready in his hands.

The wound ached, hot and sharp in the small of his back.

Hoffman descended the last few feet of slope, his horse starting a minor avalanche of small rocks and dirt. He pulled up at the edge of the trees, hesitating. After a moment he touched heels to the horse and entered the stand.

The horse saw Slocum first. It snorted and shied sideways. Hoffman blinked, eyebrows raised, eyes snapping from Slocum to the white bundle hanging from the short tree limb and back again.

"Son of a bitch," he said. "I kinda figgered it was you. How come you ain't run?"

"This is as far as I go for right now."

"Could be it's as far as you get." Hoffman eyed Slocum's rifle. He licked his lips.

Slocum said, "Got a question for you. What do they want with the girl? Or is it that the women are so ugly up here everything else looks good?"

"Don't you fret about that girl. We'll take care of her."

"Why that girl? Why not a different one?"

"Because she fits. What's that thing up there in the tree?"

"It's up there so the bears won't get it," Slocum said. "Look, I've got a message I want you to give to Deward for me."

Hoffman laughed. "You expect me to listen to you and then just go back and tell him something?"

"You'll tell him something," Slocum said. "But you won't have to go back to do it."

Slocum saw the man's face darken as the meaning of the words got through. "Listen," Hoffman said. "You got any money? Maybe we can make a deal. You can turn around and get on your horse and whip on out of here. I'll set and let you go."

"And shoot me in the back."

Hoffman grinned. "Hell. You think I'd do that?"

"Or," Slocum said, "I can just kill you and do what I please."

"They'd be all over you. If not now, then later. You get in the way of Deward and his daddy, it's as good as a death warrant."

"I've seen his daddy. It'd be hard to get in that man's way, these days."

"You bastard. If you've hurt that old man—"

"He's the same as when I found him."

Hoffman glanced again at the hanging bundle.

"Go ahead," Slocum told him. "Give that sheet a yank. It'll come right off. Have a look."

Hoffman hesitated, watching the rifle. Then he leaned in the saddle, reaching with his left hand, his right held well away from his body. He grabbed the bottom edge of the sheet and tugged. The sheet fell away.

The arm, bloodless and gray, hung by the wrist, turning slowly on the end of the rope.

"Jesus!" Hoffman shrank back from it.

Slocum said, "Deward wanted to make sure he didn't lose this, so there it is."

Hoffman reached both hands for his pistols. The movement was slow and deliberate, blatant, no attempt at distraction. His glare was wild-eyed and full of hate. Slocum tipped the rifle up and shot him through the chest twice, seeing the dust jump from the man's shirt where the bullets struck.

Hoffman rocked in the saddle and the pistols dropped from his fingers. His horse wanted to bolt, and he pulled back on the reins, bracing himself against the saddle horn, eyes clamped shut. He swung a leg over and dismounted. He wavered there a moment. Then he opened his eyes and shook his head rapidly, as if two bullets were something he could shrug off. He leaned over and reached for one of the fallen pistols.

Slocum shot him twice more. Hoffman fell to one knee, tried again to grab the pistol, but got only as far as laying his hand upon it before his body quit him. He sagged over the gun, then collapsed and lay still.

Never a word, never a cry. If he could have killed Slocum even in the final second of his life, he would have done it. Hoffman had died better than Tyson Halsey.

Slocum took the man's horse and left him there beneath the severed arm, which swung slowly from the tree branch.

A message. He wondered if he'd have to wait long for an answer.

8

He returned to the brush where he had rolled the body of Tyson Halsey. Tyson's horse was long gone, so he loaded the body onto Hoffman's mount, cursing as the animal shied away from the grizzly burden. Slocum lashed the body down with the rope from Hoffman's saddle.

He took it back to town.

People watched him, mute and staring from the boardwalks and windows, as he rode in. Women hustled their young children away from the sight, hushing their cries of curiosity. Slocum stopped in front of the Marshal's office, but the door was closed and the shade drawn. A loitering man in suspenders informed him that, about this time of day, Marshal Reed could usually be found playing faro at the Gold Slipper. He eyed the dangling arms and legs of the dead man, but wisely decided not to inquire as to the circumstances.

Slocum rode down the street to the saloon in question, the same one in which he had gambled his first night in Garrison. He swung down and pushed through

71

the batwing doors. Once inside, he moved away from the doorway. Silhouetted against the light from outdoors a man made an inviting target, and Slocum was feeling edgy. He stood and allowed his eyes to adjust.

Coal oil lamps burned along the walls, and a chandelier smoked above the center of the room. A long, polished bar, gaming tables in the rear. The largest of these was the faro table with its painted layout and card case and banker's box. Marshal Lacklin Reed sat sideways in front of it, a small stack of coins and copper markers before him, and next to these a bottle and a glass. Reed's position was strategic, so that no one could enter without his notice, and no one could come up behind him. Standard gunman's posture— stiff, poised, and ready. It seemed silly and useless here, in this out of the way trading town, but no doubt Reed believed himself impressive. He glanced once at Slocum, a quick study, then dismissed him and turned back to the game.

Slocum came over and stood before him. Reed did not look up.

"I got a dead man for you. A killing to report, if you're interested."

The faro dealer, having laid out the first two cards, hesitated before throwing the third, crucial card, looking from Slocum to Reed nervously. Reed gave out a long sigh of irritation and gestured for the man to go ahead. The dealer bent his head and threw the card. Reed lost, and gave the air a flick of his fingers as the dealer pulled in the bet.

Still not looking up at Slocum, Reed said, "You seem to miss the fact that I'm busy here." He began to place another round of markers, using his left hand.

"I'm interested in finding out how you feel about this one."

"Not just yet," Reed snapped. Now he did look up, his expression one of annoyance. "Drop him off at the undertaker's and I'll be over directly."

Slocum's mouth set hard and grim. His green eyes flashed. He nodded once, turned and walked back out the door, ignoring the chuckles and amused whispers of the other patrons. Outside, he unlashed the body and pulled it down from the horse. He picked it up by the waist and lugged it, the arms dangling, back through the doors, banging them open so forcefully with the dead man's head that they slammed and bounced off the opposite walls.

All laughter, all discussion ceased.

Slocum dragged the body to the faro layout and dumped it at Reed's feet.

The faro dealer stood up so fast he knocked his chair over. He retreated a few yards, eyes wide. Reed kept his seat.

Slocum said, "I'll make it real convenient for you. You don't even have to get up."

Reed, lips tight, looked at the dead man, then at Slocum. "You got a lot of brass, mister."

"Take a good look at him. If you need to, maybe you can ask one of these men in here to help you identify him."

"You the one shot him?"

"He drew on me."

"So you say. Anybody else see it happen?"

"I'll tell you what. Any of his family shows up to file a complaint, you let me know and I'll come running."

"He the guy shot that city kid the other day?"

"No. Bobby Todd did that. This one just got in the way. Now that I've made the matter clear for you, maybe you'll see yourself free to wire the sheriff. If you're not too busy bucking the tiger here."

Reed's brow furrowed; his jaws tightened. "You back off, Slocum. You just back yourself way the hell off."

"Somebody's got to do your job. If not you then somebody else."

Slocum stood there, waiting. Reed's position had been challenged, and his reaction could be violent, though Slocum doubted it. The man's smooth chin, freshly shaved and talced, glistened in the yellow lamplight; his long hair hung down his back, shining with scented oils. He would consider himself quite the picture, Slocum thought. The lady-killer, big with the country girls and the dollar whores.

At last, Reed said, "Anything else you'd like to say?"

"I've made my point."

"You've made it real clear."

Slocum, tired of the childish posturing, nudged the dead man with his foot. "Then you can do what you please with him."

Reed opened his mouth to say something else, but then a kid, sixteen or seventeen, burst into the saloon, hollering for him.

"I'm right here, boy," Reed said.

The kid came up, panting. He saw the dead man and his stare grew wide in wonder.

"What is it?" Reed barked.

"They sent me over from Collins's place. A drunk's in there busting it up."

"What drunk? Who is it?"

"They say it's Mike Porter, the mule skinner, soaked to the gills and mean as a panther. He's broke out all the windows and is commencing on the furniture."

Reed nodded once. "All right. You've told me. Now skip."

The kid nodded and bolted back out the door, presumably to return to the scene and observe further developments.

"You want to see me do my job, Mr. Slocum, come along," Reed said. "Maybe I can lay to rest any doubts you have as to my abilities."

He stood and checked the pistols in the sash at his waist, then strode to the batwing doors. There he paused and looked back. "You coming?"

The words were defiant, almost a challenge. Slocum considered it a moment. "All right," he said.

Reed pushed on through the doors. Slocum followed, and the two of them walked down the street toward the lower end of town.

"This Porter's all right when he's sober. Let him get tanked up and he's a hard case and a troublemaker. You know the type?"

Slocum said nothing, letting the man talk. Down the street came a rumble and a screech, and the tinkle of broken glass. Reed was half-smiling, his eyes bright and eager.

"Collins runs a tidy operation, but this is his own damn fault if he sold drink to Porter. He's seen this happen before, so there's no excuse for it."

Collins's place was on the west side of the road. A knot of men were in the street just outside, and from the midst of them came a balding gentleman in a boiled shirt and sleeve garters, no doubt Collins himself. He started to complain to Reed, and the Marshal waved him away and stepped past him to the saloon.

It was a narrow building, barely twenty feet wide, with the bar running the full length of the north wall. Until recently a great mirror had hung behind it, over the shelves of bottles and glasses and mugs, but now only the oak frame was in place, holding shards of broken glass at the corners like snaggled teeth. A single table remained upright, near the door. The chairs were so much kindling. In the center of the room stood a tall, lean-hipped man in buckskin and sweat-stained denim, a wide-brimmed hat shadowing his eyes. His face bristled with a tangled beard of black and gray, and his nose was flat and broad, bespeaking breakages of days past. In one large, work-gnarled hand he held a bottle of whiskey; in the other, a splintered chair leg. He stood and watched them, swaying slightly.

"Porter," Reed said. Slocum could not tell if it was a greeting or a challenge.

"Here you are, Reed," Porter said, and grinned. "I figgered you'd be around before too long."

"We're not going to do this anymore, Mike."

"You'll be taking me down and flopping me in that pissy smelling jail, I guess. Maybe I'll wrestle you first, how'll that be? Me and you a few quick throws?"

"I'm not taking you to jail this time, Mike."

Porter laughed and drank, then wiped the same hand across his forested chin. "I got a couple more chairs to bust here, then we'll go at it. Maybe your friend there can join us. I can whip both of you."

He stepped abruptly to the bar and smashed the chair leg onto the scarred surface of the bar top. He swung the leg sideways, clearing the few glasses and a bottle that had been abandoned there. He kicked at the side of the bar, twice, viciously. "She goddamned took off on me,

Reed! She run off! You know how I hated it when she done that! I swear, I see her again I'm going to snip her nose the way they do the squaws!"

"Your wife's been gone almost a year, Mike. I'm tired of this. Collins is tired of it, too."

"I don't care what nobody's tired of!" Porter shouted. He swung and hurled the chair leg toward the back of the room. It clattered off the wall. He faced Reed in a crouch, arms out, grinning again. "Come on, Marshal. Like last time, me and you. Only this time you don't get to hit me with no gun butt like you done."

Reed looked at Slocum, a long stare, and the corners of his mouth quirked up into a thin, bloodless smile. He faced Porter once more.

"Not this time, Mike."

Porter had been swinging his arms forward and back, as if in anticipation of Reed coming for him. Now he stopped. His anxious grin died.

"Reed . . . ," he said, looking perplexed. "I ain't talking about no gunplay."

Reed said, "Mr. Slocum, maybe it would be best if you moved off to the side."

"You don't need to do this," Slocum said. "He's a drunk. Put him in a cell and let him dry out."

"Move off to the side. I won't tell you again."

Porter held up a hand. "Reed, look here—"

"Pull it, Mike. Pull it or I'll bust you where you stand."

Reed was not even offering the man the satisfaction of preparing for him. He stood with his arms crossed over his chest, one leg slightly forward in a military pose. His long hair hung on his shoulders like a cape. Only his face betrayed his readiness, the jaw set and thrust grimly forward, his eyes narrowed to slits.

"You ain't got no call, Reed!" Porter said, his voice breaking with sudden panic. "We done this before, you never were mad like this!"

Reed stared.

"Shit!" Porter said. His large hand went down to his gun handle, fumbled there. The thong was still over the hammer.

Reed pulled his left-hand gun, cocked it, aimed. He squeezed off a round, the noise deafening in the tight, closed-in space of the barroom.

Porter jerked and stumbled backward two steps, grunting with the impact. A gout of blood showed on his shirt just above his belly. He looked at it, as if amazed to see something like that down there, uncertain of just what it was. Reed shot him again, and the spurt of the gun erupted another red stain on Porter's chest, an inch above the first one. Porter stumbled farther back, his knees buckling, his hands moving frantically behind him in search of something to grab, something to hold him up or break his fall. As he went down, Reed fired one last time into the thickening powder smoke, opening a small black hole in the center of Porter's forehead.

Reed stood and breathed deep the sharp odor of the burnt black powder. He turned and trained the pistol on Slocum's chest.

"You see it? Did you see it plain?"

Slocum regarded him, regarded the black, polished surface of the barrel and the brass frame behind it, and Reed's steady, untrembling hand. "I saw it."

"I hope you watched close. I hope you learned something."

"I learned enough."

"Good. Because you're not going to get a second chance to figure it out."

Slocum turned then and stepped through the door into the glare of the street, half expecting Reed to holler after him, to hear the blast of the gun and feel the piercing thud of the lead ball as it tore into his back. Half expecting, but only half, and it didn't come.

Collins waited outside, and with him the others, whey-faced and suddenly silent.

"What happened in there? All that shooting, did Porter pull a gun on the Marshal?"

Slocum said, "Marshal Reed was giving me a lesson in police work."

9

Early the next morning Slocum sat with his back against a tree on the slope overlooking Joshua Halsey's cabin. Below him the house was a miniature, its rough edges softened by distance and the morning haze. Off somewhere to his left was the soothing sound of rushing water over rounded stones, and the screech of the jays punctuated the ever-present chirruping of the smaller, softer birds. A rooster crowed, tardily. Slocum sat and watched.

Chickens fussed aimlessly about the dooryard, and the hogs rooted at their feed. In the corral the swaybacked horse stood with head lowered and one leg bent in rest, tail lazily switching.

Inside the cabin, Joshua Halsey lay sick and dying. Everybody on the mountain, Lorine had said, knew about her daddy and was worried. They would be worried more after finding Hoffman, and Rory's arm hanging in the trees above him. It was possible they would come here and try to take Joshua away to a safer spot.

Slocum wondered if Lacklin Reed knew about old Joshua, if he was worried.

The thought came to his mind, unbidden.

For some reason Reed did not want Slocum muddying the countryside with his tracks, and it might be only a territorial concern, like one dog who resents another dog pissing on the same fences. But it could be much more than that. Slocum had heard nothing from Reed after the killing of the teamster; there had been no appearance to underscore the lesson dealt out in that gloomy saloon, no further warnings. The lesson had contained no specifics, only the broad order to back off.

He wondered if Lacklin Reed ever came here.

The birds left off singing, suddenly. The girl was down the slope, behind him. He could hear her, picking her way carefully through the pine needles. He had seen her come out of the house earlier, fresh and in a clean dress as yellow as the sun. He had watched her come around the base of the slope, holding her skirts up away from the ground with one hand. She had disappeared around the hill, and then a few minutes later he'd heard her climbing toward him. She would have found his horse down there, tethered to a deadfall in a draw behind a stand of dead brush. He drew his pistol and laid it on the hard-packed earth beside him.

"Come around here and sit down, Lorine."

The crunch of the needles then, all caution gone now from the steps. She appeared from around the tree, a half smile on her face, like a child caught in a game. "How'd you know it was me?"

"A body could hear you a mile off."

Her face cinched up into a pout, and she flopped down beside him and leaned against the tree. She put her legs straight out, feet together. They were bare and powdered with fine dust from her climb.

Slocum put the pistol away. "You're going to get sap on your dress."

She shrugged, as if this did not concern her. "What are you doing here, resting like a lazy man?"

"Waiting."

"For my brothers." She breathed deeply, let it out. "If they come, what are you going to do, shoot them?"

"If they come, are you going to warn them I'm here?"

She looked at him. "I don't like them very much. If you wanted to take shots at the bunch of them I wouldn't do a thing to stop it."

She plucked a piece of grass growing through the carpet of dead pine needles beside her and fiddled with it in her two hands, her head down and her feet wagging back and forth. She'd washed her hair this morning, and Slocum could smell the soap on her.

"These people they killed," she said. "They friends of yours?"

"Not really."

"Then how come you want to shoot them for it?"

Slocum sidestepped the question. "Is Marshal Reed scared of your brothers?"

"Everybody is scared of my brothers. Especially Lacklin Reed. My brothers run him. Or Deward does. You watch out for Deward, John Slocum. He's the bad one. Bobby Todd and the others, they just do what Deward tells them to do, or what they think he wants them to do. Deward is the thinker, the one who plans everything. He's trying to please my daddy, who don't know nothing anymore."

"How is your daddy today?"

"About the same. Deward came to see him last night. Tried to talk to him, told him he was going to have him right again real soon, he had a plan. What kind of plan could he have for a thing like that?"

Slocum did not want to venture a guess, but he had a gut feeling that whatever the plan was, it included Julia Conway.

The old man was still here. Deward had not taken him away.

Lorine said, "My daddy's going to stay the way he is forever, and I'm going to have to take care of him until I'm just as old and worn out as he is."

"Don't you have any beaus?"

She looked at him, chin raised. "I've had a few." Her head went back down, and she sighed. "Most of them were just trash. Their hands are always dirty and they just want to paw me around. Most of them are some kind of kin and I don't even know how. My momma told me that your babies can come out mush-brained if you . . . if you do it with close kin. I don't want that. Deward used to push them on me, and tell me if they was kin they was good enough for anybody and that I shouldn't put myself above my own people. He'd hit me, too."

"Does Deward hit you a lot?"

"Sometimes. And if he gets too bad I run off." She looked at him. Her face brightened. "You want to see where I go? Come on."

She jumped up and reached for his hand. He allowed her to pull him up, and she led the way back down the hill, away from the house, past Slocum's tethered horse, to where the hills came together in a dry streambed. She led him along this wash, her naked feet kicking up puffs of dust as she hurried forward, her tiny hand still grasping his.

They went perhaps a quarter mile, to where the bank of the wash had collapsed. She clambered over, and on the other side stood what looked at first glance to be just a tumble of brush. On closer inspection Slocum saw that the brush had been carefully placed on a lashed frame of sticks and old lumber.

She ducked down and went through the narrow opening. It was low enough that Slocum would have to remove his hat. He held back, and she tugged at his hand.

"Come on. This is my special place. I built it myself. It's where I go to get away from them."

Slocum ducked his head and entered. Within the shelter of the brush it was neat and comfortable and cool, with a blanket spread on the ground and a stack of books next to the earthen bank. He had to lower himself to his knees to prevent his head from banging against the brush roof. A picture was pressed, frame and all, into the bank, a tintype showing a dark-haired woman staring straight ahead, her mouth grim and her hair pulled back. She resembled Lorine. Her eyes were large and haunted.

"Your mother?"

She nodded. "Deward threw it out in the yard one day, after she died. I brung it here to keep it safe."

"Deward and your other brothers, do they know about this hidey?"

"They never come here, but I don't guess they look too hard for me, neither."

"Why do they treat you so bad?"

She sat down in the middle of the shelter, cross-legged, and smoothed her dress over her legs. "My momma wasn't their momma. Theirs died, back before the War. Joshua married my momma and then I come along, but they never liked her, and they don't consider me real kin, since I come from her."

She reached up for his hand and pulled on it, bringing him down to her.

"I never brung nobody here before. I never wanted to, not till I seen you ride into the yard yesterday."

He sat down beside her, and she leaned into him, resting her head against his shoulder.

"Sometimes I get so very tired. I just want someone to take care of me."

He stroked her hair, feeling the softness of it, the sleek animal warmth. Her arms came up around him, clinging, desperately insistent. He lay her down on the blanket, gently, and she looked up at him, her lips parted and her eyes hungry.

"You can unbutton my dress if you want," she said.

The buttons were in the front. Slocum unfastened them, working his way down to the last one, just above her flat belly, and peeled the dress back to expose her small breasts. She cupped them with her hands and pressed them together, offering them to him.

He tossed his hat away. He leaned down and pressed his mouth to her right breast, flicking at the budlike nipple with his tongue. She arched her back, the suck of her breath sharp and sudden.

"Oh, God, oh yes, John Slocum."

His hand traveled down the flat plane of her belly, pushing the fabric away. She wore nothing down there beneath the dress, and he felt the downy patch of hair. As his finger traveled through it into the moist softness of her inner lips, she cried out and her hips jerked. He moved his hand away, thinking that he was going too quickly for her. She grabbed it and pressed it back into herself, guiding his finger deeper inside. Her neck bent back, and she moaned low in her throat. He stroked in and out gently, feeling her quiver under his hand. Her musk began to permeate the air.

"Oh, Jesus, that is so good, so good," she breathed. Her hips began to rotate with the motion of his finger, urging him to faster movements, harder, and her breathing quickened, each breath shorter and more demanding. The cry began, moving it seemed from the channel in which his finger worked and up through her, into her throat, fluttering; and then she was bucking against his hand, gasping, crying louder, her hips bouncing up from the blanket. Slocum stayed with her until the spasms subsided, and then she was up and ripping at the buttons of his shirt, at his pants.

"I want you," she said. "Oh, God I want you now, John. Hurry, please, I want you inside me."

When she had him stripped, she pushed him back on the blanket and ran her mouth from his chest down the ridges of his muscled stomach. He gasped as her mouth found his swollen member and sank down over it, hot and hungry. She played her tongue from base to tip over and again, moving faster and more eagerly, then slowing, nipping with her teeth and pressing her lips hard against the tip, pressing hard and down, down the length, lips taut, tongue flicking, until she had taken the whole of him. Then back up, and down once more, agonizingly slow. Slocum stroked her face, feeling her cheeks and the tight circle of her lips where they met him. He groaned, hips churning.

She tortured him, deliciously, until he throbbed and swelled nearly to the bursting point. She released him then and moved up, mounting him as she would mount a horse, positioning herself over his shaft and sinking down on him.

Her channel was tight and wet and even hotter than her mouth had been. She took all of him in one motion, a sudden and hard thrusting. Her head fell back and her mouth opened in a soundless scream as she sat there quivering against him. Then she began to move.

Slowly at first, up and down his shaft, her juices spilling over him, and then more quickly, her hands digging into his hip bones, pulling him into her. He drove, up and deep, thrusting as she demanded, feeling her muscles slick and rippling around him, milking him.

He paced himself to stay with her. Her movements became more frantic, wilder. Their wet skin slapped together, and with every thrust she moaned as his full, rigid length slipped into her again and again and again, endlessly, until at last the cry started once more. He could feel it begin from the base of his cock, as if coming from deep within himself as well, moving up through him into her, and she slammed herself fully down onto him as he burst and flooded into her. She fell against him and held him as the eruption took them, shook them.

He stayed hard, and when the spasms had passed, he moved her over onto her back, still inside her. Her channel pulsed around him, gripping, and as he began again, stroking into her, she rolled back and her legs came up and twined around his waist. He pumped, slamming into her, and she reached to meet him with every stroke, mouth open and panting, eyes screwed tightly shut. Her tight little tunnel was a cauldron boiling with their mingled juices. Her coming seemed constant, endless; she went wild under him, hips jerking and roiling beneath his violent thrusts, and she screamed. This time the explosion was sharper than before, needle-like, and he came in rapid spurts of white-hot pulsing fire.

Spent, they lay together for a few minutes, saying nothing. Then they dressed. Lorine said, "You think I'm bad."

"Not at all."

She buttoned her dress, looking pleased, but kept her eyes averted. "They wanted—" she began, then stopped. Began again. "They wanted me to do that, but I couldn't. Not—"

"Who did? Deward and your brothers?"

She nodded, still looking down, though her dress was buttoned now. "Yes. But not, you know, with them. They thought it might work, even though that's not what she said."

"Not what who said?"

She reached for his arm and grabbed it with both of her small hands. "With my father. They wanted me to get in bed with my own father."

"Why would they want that, Lorine?"

"Because I'm young. And the old woman told them it might help."

"What old woman? The doctor woman I've been told about?"

"I'll take you there. You'll see. You talk to her."

10

The old woman's place was a half mile down the canyon from Lorine's little brush hideaway. It was made of pine logs, painted white, with a low roof, compact and solid-looking. Chickens were there in profusion. The house faced a small clearing, but on the other three sides the trees grew closely, towering pine that loomed overhead, casting perpetual shadow.

Forty feet from the house Lorine stopped and made Slocum wait while she went to the door alone. She knocked once. Apparently there was no one inside, and Lorine went around the corner of the house, out of Slocum's view.

In a moment she returned and motioned for Slocum to follow her. The old woman was around back, tossing feed to her chickens from a bowl she held in the crook of one arm. As Slocum turned the corner, she stopped and looked at him with the coldest, deadest eyes he'd ever seen.

She was gaunt, rail thin, in a featureless gray dress and shapeless sunbonnet, the white of her hair hanging out the back in frail wisps. Her fingers were gnarled and twisted with arthritis, her face pinched and tight.

Slocum touched his hat brim and nodded. "Ma'am."

"This is Mother Agnes, John. She'll tell you."

"Tell him what, child?" the woman snapped, flinging away the remainder of the chicken feed. Her voice was rasping and raw, as if she spent every night shrieking to her gods.

"You tell him what you said about my daddy," Lorine demanded. "About what would make him well."

"You oughtn't to do this, girl. You don't bring no stranger into the business of folks on this mountain. It ain't right."

Lorine flushed, but she did not back down, nor did she lower her gaze. Her fists were clenched at her sides, as if she might at any moment strike the old woman.

Slocum said, "Lorine says you wanted her to commit incest with her father."

The woman's dead eyes flashed alight. "Evil child! I never spoke such words!"

"Then you tell him what you said, what you told my brothers to make them think that!"

"One of your brothers was here three days ago and I had to take off his arm because he'd been shot. You should be more hurtful about that, less about what I said. And I believe the man who shot him was named John."

"I don't care," Lorine said.

"And when Tyson left here yesterday, I heard shots, and I felt a bad feeling in the air. The same bad feeling I get when I look at you and this man here."

"I don't care, Mother Agnes. I don't care if they all get shot or ride off or get blown up, because they're bad, all of them, just bad!"

"Girl, how you talk." Mother Agnes stepped forward and pointed a bent finger at Lorine. "And I smell things too, girl. I smell your womanness, and the odor of man on you. You rut like a pig and then dare to come here and preach to me about who's bad and who isn't, and you tell lies about me."

Lorine pushed the old woman's finger away. "I ain't told no lies! Deward shoved me right up to Daddy's bed and shouted for me to climb into it, and he swore if Daddy died it would be my fault because I refused him. He said you told him it would make him well to have a young girl love him!"

"A girl. Not you. Deward twists my words."

"Then tell her what your words were," Slocum said. "Answer her."

"It's not for a young girl's ears."

"Neither is what Deward told her, but he made sure she heard it. What about her father?"

"I help the people on this mountain," Mother Agnes growled, her eyes coming back to life, the spark of a black fire flashing from far back behind the milky irises. "I help them the same as I've helped them all my life, from the time we was in Tennessee together until now. They trust me, and I stand by their trust. They brung me out here in a wagon with a canvas cover. Took us two months, but they brung me because they trusted me, and needed me. I mend their breaks and lay poultices on their hurts and lance their boils, and if I answer to anyone it will be to them, not to some puffed-up gunman. Not to some rutting stranger."

"They trust you, but you couldn't help Joshua Halsey."

"I told them what had to be done. I seen what was in the signs, and I told Deward what he must find and how it must come to pass. Them words was for him and his family."

"*I* am his family!" Lorine said.

"Only part, girl. You are of the second line."

Lorine flushed scarlet. She turned away, ready to burst into tears of frustration and anger. She strode off a few feet, head down, her small body trembling.

Slocum said, "You told Deward to find a girl to get in bed with the old man, that this would bring him back to life."

"What I told him was for his ears, gunman."

"You told him to find a girl with a white streak in her hair."

She rocked backward, as if from a physical blow. Her color, already pale and washed out, went even more pasty, and the dark fire in her old eyes faded, replaced by undisguised fear.

"Who told you that? Deward wouldn't tell you."

"He told me, but not in words."

"Joshua Halsey is old, and he's failing. He must have the life juices in him resurrected and flowing back to his heart and his liver and his brain. It's all that can save him, because those juices are what drove him all his life. He's lost his manliness, and that's why he's ailing."

"Where do you see these signs, Grandma? How do you come up with a girl who has a streak of white in her hair? Do you dream it, or do voices whisper it to you?"

"Mock me as you please, gunman. I see what's there to see."

Slocum pushed harder. "Do they pay you for what you see? Do they give you money for these visions?"

She stiffened, threw her head back. "They give me what they can afford to give; I don't ask. Food, lamp oil, wood for my stove. I don't need a lot."

"If they gave you so much as a penny, then I'd say you cheated them, old woman."

Lorine whirled and placed a hand on Slocum's arm. "John, no! Don't—"

Slocum said, "She's been filling all of your heads with her back hills magic, Lorine. Her little vision is what caused that ruckus down there on the prairie, what made Bobby Todd blow that boy's brains out."

"John, please—"

"*I seen what was there, gunman!*" Mother Agnes shrieked. "I see it there the way my mother taught me to see it, the way her mother taught her, and her mother before that!" She whirled, dropping the bowl, and caught up a squawking, speckled hen. The bird beat its wings uselessly in mindless fright, sending bits of down and feathers into the air. She grasped it by its horny legs and held it upside down and from the pocket of her dress produced a short-bladed knife with a bone handle. She slit the chicken's belly open in one smooth motion. The blood dripped freely onto the ground, some of it spattering on the old woman's dress as the chicken writhed in its death throes.

"Oh, God," Lorine said, and backed away in horror. Slocum stayed where he was, face grim.

Mother Agnes reached into the cut and pulled out the slick entrails. She freed them from the chicken's body with a quick jerk and tossed them on the ground at Slocum's boots, then flung the bird away from her, where it thrashed out what was left of its life in a patch of tall brush.

The entrails steamed.

"There, gunman, that's where I see it, in there!" She pointed with a gnarled finger, jabbing the air. Her face was a mask of contorted wrath, her mouth ugly and lipless, twisted down to show the dark stumps of her bottom teeth.

"You gut a chicken," Slocum said, "and this gives you a vision."

"You see there how they fall!" she shouted, pointing. "Every coil, every twist there has a meaning! It's all there for them that knows how to see it!"

"You see something there now, old woman?"

"Oh, yes," she said. She smiled and crossed her arms. "Oh, my yes. I see your death there, gunman. I see it plain as day. You'll die on this mountain. And soon."

11

They headed back through the trees, toward Lorine's hideaway, walking through the dust among the pine needles and dead cones and gray, naked rocks. Lorine was shaken and moved with her hands cupping her elbows, arms closely in, hugging herself.

"It doesn't mean anything," Slocum told her. "Some crazy old woman looks at a bunch of innards and chants off a prediction. It's all playacting."

She shook her head, walking along and refusing to look at him. "No," she said. "You don't know. Everything she says comes true, John. She knows things; she really sees them. A cousin of ours got killed by the Cheyenne on a hunting trip, and she seen that was going to happen. She warned him not to go. She knew Daddy was going to get sick. She told Deward it was fixing to happen and said that Daddy should get his business squared away. She knows things."

"Lorine—"

Still she would not look at him. She walked as if cold, the prediction of Slocum's death having touched her with the chill of the grave. She had already written him off as gone, Slocum thought. She was walking through the trees with a dead man.

They were a few hundred yards from the Halsey place, just over a short rise, in a hollow where the pines grew thick and darkened the mountain floor. One great tree had been blasted by lightning perhaps a century ago, and canted off at a severe angle about fifteen feet above their heads.

Slocum sensed the movement before he actually saw it. There it was, a flicking of light and shadow between the pines.

He grabbed Lorine's shoulder with his left hand, stopping her. She looked up at him, startled, and he pulled her around behind him, his right hand moving down to the butt of his Colt.

"Pull it one inch out of that holster and you're dead meat, Slocum."

Slocum froze.

A cackling, high-pitched voice. It came again, this time in the form of a laugh. Bobby Todd Halsey emerged from the trees carrying a Winchester rifle, his chinless mouth agape with anxious mirth, his eyes eager and predatory.

"You stay behind me," Slocum told Lorine.

Next to Bobby Todd came a gangly man with a wispy beard, armed with an old caplock rifle. He looked curious and eager, eyes moving back and forth from Slocum to Bobby Todd. Slocum remembered him from the fight back at the camp, an ineffectual sort who had sat his horse and watched.

Bobby Todd said, "Looky here what we got, Jason. You burn a man and he still don't learn. Mr. Trickshot who is so damn good at shooting the arms off defenseless men."

Jason laughed, a sucking, snuffling sound. "He has got your baby sister, Bobby."

"I see he does. Lorine, you step away from him. Get your ass back down there where Daddy's at. He's needing you about now."

"Bobby Todd," Lorine shouted, "just go on and leave us alone! Please!"

"You heard me, girl. Step off from him. You don't need to be concerned about his welfare, honey. He's the one shot Rory's arm off, and probably done for Tyson. And Cleve Hoffman, too. Rory died last night. Did you know that, girl? The poison from his cut-off arm swole up in him, and he died."

Lorine put her hands to her face.

"This man is killing your family off bit by bit, and I am going to square it."

"No!" Lorine yelled. Bobby Todd jerked his head at Jason, motioning for the man to go over and get her.

"Fetch his pistol out, too, while you're at it. Be careful. He is a slick son of a bitch." To Slocum he called, "You stand tall there, boy. I will drill you dead center."

Jason left his rifle against a tree and minced over, wary. He freed Slocum's pistol from its holster and tossed it behind him toward Bobby Todd. Then, still careful of Slocum, he reached for Lorine. She sidled away from him.

"Goddamn it, Lorine," Bobby Todd shouted, "behave!"

Slocum wanted to lance out with a boot and bust the other man's knee for him; it was right there and he could have done it in a single motion, but Bobby Todd was anxious with the rifle. Jason caught Lorine's arm and dragged her, swinging and kicking, toward the trees. She slipped and fell to her knees in the pine needles, and when Jason raised a hand to slap her, Slocum moved as if to go after him. Bobby Todd made a cautioning noise.

"You're going to give me an excuse to do it fast, and that ain't as much fun," Bobby Todd said.

"No need to hurt her."

"Let me decide that. Jason, you take her back down to the house and put her inside. When you come back, fetch along my rope from the barn."

Jason yanked Lorine to her feet and pulled her away. They disappeared through the trees.

"You been diddling that, have you?" Bobby Todd asked. When Slocum didn't answer, he went on. "I guess since you grabbed hold of my sister, it'll be all right when I go down and get that woman of yours. Fair trade and everything."

Slocum stared at him.

"I figured you to run like a damn rabbit," Bobby Todd said. "Anybody with any smarts would have. But hell no, you got to shoot a damn fine horse out from under me, and then take that girl back. You caused us a lot of fret, boy. I guess a little mark with a hot iron ain't enough for you. We're going to have to do the whole job."

Jason returned bearing a coil of soft and dirty cotton rope, claiming it was all he could find down there. Bobby Todd said it would do. Jason handed the rope over and then picked up his gun. It was an ancient Hawken, the bore of the .50-caliber barrel as wide and black as a train tunnel. Jason looked serious about things now, still panting from his hurried trip up the slope, but no longer grinning.

Bobby Todd put his arm through the coils of rope and moved to Slocum with the Winchester held across his chest. He got close enough for Slocum to smell the dried sweat on him, and the stale odor of his clothes. Dirt was caked into the cracks and lines of the man's hands.

Bobby Todd said, "He moves wrong, you put that ball through his face."

Jason nodded curtly, raised the rifle and cocked it.

Slocum gathered saliva in his mouth to spit, but before he could get it done, Bobby Todd raised the butt of the rifle and slammed it against the side of Slocum's head.

Slocum went down, feeling the pine needles crackling under him, the prod of rocks and old pinecones. The world went hazy, and a balloon of numbness swelled out from his left ear. His arms moved sluggishly as he brought them up over his head, trying to protect himself against the next blow, which he knew must be coming.

Someone grabbed his arms and jerked them roughly, outstretched. A boot shoved him over onto his back and pressed him flat against the ground. Tightness around his wrists, jerking hard, and then Bobby Todd's voice, sharp and loud, "Get it up over that bend. Come on, throw it, don't be so goddamned feeble!"

He felt the rasping vibrations through the rope as it was drawn over the coarse bark of the bent pine. His head cleared, and he realized what was happening. As the line grew taut and he was pulled to his feet, he managed to reach forward and grab the rope and take a strain on it so that his hands would not be pulled off at the wrists when the rope took his weight.

Jason was doing the work of hoisting him, but Slocum's weight was almost too much for the scrawny man. Bobby Todd came over to help, and the two of them leaned into it. Slocum was hauled upward, his elbows and shoulders screaming at him, his muscles straining against the pull. They yanked him until his boots were five feet above the ground, then tied the rope off on the trunk of a pine.

"Gather the wood," Bobby Todd said. "Plenty of it around here. We want to make it a big one."

Jason scurried to find chunks and branches of dead wood and began piling it beneath Slocum's feet. Bobby Todd helped, moving slowly, easily, happy and confident with Slocum dangling over him, helpless. He piled dead branches and pinecones and dry brush. When the pyre was sufficient, he dug a Lucifer match from his shirt pocket, raked it to life on his pant leg and set it to the brush.

The flames licked up through the tangled branches, the pine, dry as powder, catching fast. Slocum thrashed at the end of the rope, testing the swing, the tautness, what movement he was allowed. He felt distant heat through the soles of his boots and low on his legs. The bend in the tree over which the rope was pulled stood too high for him to swing up to it.

Bobby Todd craned his neck. "How you feeling? Getting warm up there yet?" He laughed, and turned to look at Jason to get him to laugh along with him. Jason stared, grimly, at Slocum and at the fire beginning to dance more wildly beneath him.

"You're going to die, Slocum," Bobby Todd said. "But, man, you are going to die slow. You're gonna have plenty of time to think about Rory and Tyson and Cleve Hoffman, and before it's over I'm going to hear you scream their names over and over again."

The sweat trickled from Slocum's wrists and down his arms. His shoulders, upper arms, upper back, were a solid mass of pain, and the sweat was in his eyes, droplets of it dangling from his chin. He felt his boot soles warming, the heat growing and becoming almost palpable, traveling up his legs, over his knees and into his thighs, a blanket of warmth gaining intensity, growing more fierce. He began to swing himself forward and back—a feeble attempt to keep from staying in one place, where he would roast to death—trying to put off the inevitable for as long as he could. The movement made Bobby Todd giggle like a child.

A bush caught strong, flared up, lashing at Slocum's legs. A thick branch caught and roared, the gasses hissing and going up with a whoosh. He heard the snap and pop as the pine started burning in earnest, the sap inside turning to steam and bursting, the smoke thickening and burning his nostrils. His eyes watered. His pant legs grew hotter and hotter, and he wondered how long before they burst into flame and encased his lower body in a sheath of fire. He wondered if he would scream, and for how long.

A rifle shot cracked against the blaze.

"Bobby Todd! Jason! You cut him down! Now!"

Lorine's voice. Slocum craned to look. She stood at the edge of the trees, holding Slocum's rifle.

Jason, wide-eyed, took a single step toward the rope.

"Don't you do it, Jason," Bobby Todd snapped. "Lorine! You put that rifle down or I'm going to whip you!"

He moved as if to come after her, and she sent a bullet past his ear.

"Drop your guns, both of you, or I'll shoot you where you stand!"

Jason complied immediately, tossing the Hawken away as if it had become suddenly as hot as the fire before him. Bobby Todd eyed his half sister as she cocked the rifle and trained the barrel on him.

"Throw it down, Bobby Todd! I swear to God I'll kill you!"

He saw that she meant it. The certainty of it was in her stance, in the rock-still way in which she held the rifle. The sudden flash of retribution for the years of abuse and meanness was only a muzzle blast away. He tossed the Winchester down.

"You're going to be sorry you done this, girl, going against your own people."

"Cut him down!"

Jason hurried to the tree, knife out, and sawed away at the cotton rope.

It gave with a snap. The tightness broke, and Slocum hurtled down into the fire. He hit with both feet, felt the burning mass crumble beneath him and threw himself off to the cool ground. He landed on his shoulder and rolled, kicking his legs against the dirt to snuff the burning places on his clothes.

Jason and Bobby Todd ran. They crashed through the trees in different directions, both with their heads down and shoulders hunched, in case Lorine should fire after them.

But she let them go. She rushed to Slocum's side, and with the knife Jason had dropped, she sawed at the rope around Slocum's chafed wrists, calling to him, pleading with him to please be all right.

When his hands were free, he staggered to the nearest tree and leaned against it, gasping. He rubbed his wrists where the rope had torn them and watched as the fire raged upward, over the spot where he had hung.

He allowed Lorine to lead him to the house. She fetched him a bucket of water. He drank deeply.

"You've got to leave," she told him. "He'll be back, and he'll bring the others with him."

"What about you?"

"Later it might go hard for me. They won't hurt me now. They need me here to take care of Daddy."

"Leave him. Let them tend him. I'll take you into town with me. You'll be safe there."

The way she shook her head told Slocum there was no give in her on this point. "I have to stay. They wouldn't know how to take care of him. He's my daddy, too."

12

Her father had told her only that there could be trouble on the street at any time, and ordered her to stay in her room.

Julia had protested.

"Damn it, girl," Mr. Conway said, "if you insist on staying here, you'll have to cooperate."

"Cooperate at what, Dad? You're not doing anything."

Mr. Conway's round, blunt face blazed red, the way it always did when he grew angry—which, the past few months, was more and more often. He'd been under a great strain, and Julia suspected he was nearly broke. Things in Chicago were in a slump, and Mr. Conway had too much money invested and not enough coming back in. Still, he insisted on living as if nothing were wrong. Putting on a show. Even this hunting trip was a show, planned for months and taken even though he could no longer afford it. Let them know you are down, he'd said once, and they'll kick you to pieces.

Now he said, "Slocum is handling it." She could

smell the whiskey on his breath.

"John is handling it for himself, not for you. Not for me."

"He's handling it. If someone else is doing your work for you, you let him do it. He's going to take care of those men, and I'm going to be here when he does it. For the moment you're staying inside, and I'm going down to the saloon on the corner and make more inquiries about these people. Maybe when he gets back I'll have something he can use."

He whipped out of her room and away, and as his footsteps faded down the hallway, it came to her that her father had perhaps gone a little crazy. It made her feel lost and lonely.

She lay down on the bed and thought about John Slocum and wondered where he was. A strange man, handsome in a rugged sort of way, with a strong jaw and the coldest, harshest green eyes she could ever remember having seen. And yet those rough hands could be so gentle, so sure and confident. She remembered how it had felt, having his solid, muscled body pressed against hers, the feel of him inside her, and she shivered.

And she wanted him there. Not just for the physical comfort. There were too many of those men out there, the grizzled, sweating Halseys. Slocum could not get them all, and she was afraid they would come for her again while he was gone, and her father could do nothing to stop them.

She felt shaky and brittle, much as she had after the trouble in Chicago—but not nearly as bad. In Chicago she had felt totally alone and helpless; here, though she was miles away from everything familiar to her, home and friends, there was something real she could cling to—a man had fought for her, and would fight for her again, she was certain, if the need arose.

She heard loud voices from the lobby downstairs. With her heart suddenly pounding hard in her throat, she went to the door and opened it a crack to listen.

"I'm the Marshal, for God's sake," someone said, "I just want to check on her. Now which room is it?"

At the front desk. The desk clerk, in a high and nervous voice, replied, "It would hardly be proper, sir. She's an unmarried young lady, I can't let a man—"

"Damn it," the Marshal said, "you're not listening to me."

"Yes, I am, Marshal Reed, but Miss Conway isn't to be bothered. Mr. Slocum told me—"

"Slocum? Slocum be damned! He doesn't run this town—I do. Hand me that register book."

Julia went out to the landing and stood looking down at the front desk. "I'm Julia Conway," she said. "Who are you and what do you want?"

The man in the lobby was tall and well dressed, with thin, sharp features and shoulder-length hair. His mustache was full and neatly trimmed. But his eyes were small and somehow predatory, and when he put them on her, she wanted to turn and run. She fought off the urge.

He nodded. "Lacklin Reed, ma'am. City Marshal. I was told you'd had some trouble, and I wanted to make sure you were all right."

"As you can see I'm fine."

"Yes, ma'am, I sure see that." The small eyes glittered. He rested his hands on the twin revolvers he wore in the red sash around his waist. "Your friend Mr. Slocum asked me to check on you. Is he around by any chance?"

"If you had talked to John Slocum you'd know where he was."

"It's been a few minutes. I've lost track of him."

"I thank you for your concern, Marshal Reed. Everything here is under control. If we need you, we'll call for you."

Reed touched the flat brim of his hat. "You make sure you do that, ma'am."

The desk clerk was staring up at Julia. Reed took advantage of the distraction to grab the register book and scan it. The clerk made a flustered move to reclaim it, but Reed raised a finger and poked him in the chest, and the clerk shrank back. When he was finished, Reed stepped away from the desk and once more touched his hat brim. His eyes held a triumphant look. He went to the front door and out.

When Slocum came in, it was nearly dusk, and Mr. Conway met him on the hotel porch.

"Well?" he demanded.

Slocum resisted the impulse to shove the man out of his way and walk on. He was tired and sore, and his patience was ebbing fast. "Mr. Conway, you're beginning to irritate me."

"Are those killers still alive?"

Slocum took a deep breath. "Not as many of them."

"Are you going out after them again?"

"Mr. Conway, get your daughter and meet me in my room in half an hour. I have some words for you." Before the round little man could say anything else, Slocum stepped past him and went up the stairs.

In his room he stripped off his sweaty, smoke-stained clothing and washed. He changed into his only other pair of jeans and donned a fresh shirt, and by the time the knock came at his door, he was once more presentable.

He opened the door and Julia rushed to him. "Oh, John," she said, pressing her face to his chest. "I'm so glad you're back. You can't believe how worried I was."

Mr. Conway stared.

After a moment Slocum removed himself from Julia's embrace and led her to a chair. "Mr. Conway, come in and sit down," he said. He gestured to the bed.

When the man was settled, Slocum said, "I've asked you once to leave here, and I am asking it again."

"Never," Conway said.

"I've learned a few things today. Your daughter figures mightily in the plans of these people, and I'd rather she wasn't around to tempt them."

"John—" Julia said.

"We've been all through this, Slocum," Conway said.

"Yes," Slocum said. "But there's more to it than we first thought. It's not just men who want a pretty girl."

Conway said, "There's no point—"

"Yes, there is, Dad," Julia said. "This concerns me and I have a right to know. What is it, John?"

Mr. Conway glared. Slocum ignored him and softly related what he had learned, using the most gentle terms he could for such a barbaric thing: the dying father and the old witch woman's cure.

Conway went pale. "Julia," he said. "Leave us."

She opened her mouth to protest.

"Leave us, I said. Now."

She nodded finally and rose, giving Slocum a worried look before going out the door and closing it behind her. When she was gone, Mr. Conway placed his hands on his knees and leaned forward.

"I do not appreciate you telling my daughter such things."

"She's a grown woman. Like she said, it involved her, and she had a right to know."

"She's not a well girl, Slocum. She's not in any condition to have a say in what she does or does not need to know. It's one of the reasons we came on this trip in the first place, to give her a chance to clear her mind."

"Clear her mind of what?"

"She's been through a lot in the last year. She was involved with a man, and he betrayed her. There was an incident. She took it hard."

"How hard?"

"It nearly unbalanced her. And then this vicious murder, her own cousin killed in front of her eyes."

"Then take her out of here, Conway. Take her and go home."

Conway covered his face with his hands, scrubbed them up and down. "I can't, Slocum. I can't leave this unfinished."

"You poor bastard," Slocum said. "It's not yours to finish."

"Then you finish it! But I'm not leaving here until you do! I can't go back home with those killers still loose. Finish it for me, Slocum, please!"

Slocum stared at him and said nothing.

Conway slammed the door behind him.

13

Later Slocum sat at the small writing desk in the corner and disassembled and cleaned the Navy Colt, wiping each part down with an oiled rag, then replaced the powder and ball in each chamber and thumbed on percussion caps. With the pistol near at hand on the table, he cleaned and oiled the Henry rifle. His face was grim as he worked. When the knock came, he picked up the pistol and carried it with him to the door.

Julia entered, closed the door quickly behind her and leaned against it. Her hair was down, held at the back of her neck with a green ribbon. The top button at the throat of her dress was undone. She was flushed and breathing deeply.

"Do you always answer the door with a gun in your hand?" she asked.

"Not always," Slocum said. "Just often enough to stay alive." He laid the pistol back down on the desk. "If your father knew you were here, it could cause an ugly scene."

"Nobody saw me. Are you sorry I came?"

"I'm very happy you came. But I want you to do me a favor."

"I want to do you lots of favors."

"Tell me what happened in Chicago."

For a moment he thought she would not speak. She pressed herself harder against the door and closed her eyes. Slocum waited.

"I was in love with a man," she said at last. "His name was Tom. It turned out that he was not so deeply in love with me as I had thought, and I learned he was seeing someone else. The daughter of a man more rich and important than my father. And so I went to him and threatened to expose him."

"And what did he do?"

"He . . . abducted me."

Again Slocum waited. She opened her eyes and looked at him. After a moment she took a deep breath and went on.

"He said he couldn't afford to let me do it. He was going to marry this woman and her father was going to give him a position high up in the family business. If I opened my mouth about us it would ruin everything. He took me by force to the stockyards. He had a gun and meant to kill me, and toss me into one of the cattle pens to be trampled until no one would recognize me when I was finally found."

"What happened?"

"There are railroad tracks running through there. A man at the switchyard saw us, and followed. He had an iron bar in his hand, something they use when they switch the tracks around. He accosted Tom, and when Tom fired at him and missed, the man hit him with the bar and killed him."

"In front of you."

She nodded stiffly. "Yes."

"And you were a while getting over it."

"I don't know that I'll ever get over it, John. I ran until I thought my heart would beat itself right out of my chest. Somebody found me and brought me home. I stayed in my room for months, refusing to come out, not even for the inquest. They sent a man over to take my statement and write it down."

"And now this."

She nodded again. "Satisfied?"

"But your father still refuses to take you out of here."

"My father is fighting his own demons. He's afraid to run from them, because if he starts running he's afraid he may never stop."

She left the door and walked to him. She offered her hands, and Slocum took them, and she leaned against him.

"And I can understand a little of that. Because if I run from you, John, I'll never be able to love any man, ever. Do you understand?"

She lifted her face to be kissed, and Slocum did so, softly, reassuringly. Her hands came up on his back and gripped him to her fiercely, and her kiss grew heated. Her mouth opened and her tongue darted, moist and warm and entreating. She broke away, gasping.

"I need this, John. I need it as I need breath itself. My father thinks he knows what's right and good for me, but he doesn't. I know what will heal me."

He carried her to the bed, laid her down on it and opened the buttons down the front of her dress. He freed her breasts and kissed the pink nipples.

"Yes," she hissed, her back arching. "Yes, it's what I need."

He stripped her hurriedly, then himself. She sat up on the bed, ready to come to him, to take frantic charge of their lovemaking, and Slocum put a hand on her right breast and gently pushed her back down.

"No. Lay still."

"I can't," she gasped, gripping his wrist.

"Yes you can. Hush now." He kept his hand on her breast until she quieted, then tongued his way from her breasts down to the matted darkness of her channel. Each time she struggled to move, he pressed her gently back into the bed, shushed her, stroked her until she calmed and then resumed kissing the soft mound, tonguing at her clitoris and feeling her hips twitch in response—the good response, not the desperate jerking of the need to escape. He kissed his way down her inner thighs, then back up again, smelling her deep musk. Her fingers curled into his hair, gripping him, trying to pull him up to her.

When he was certain she was ready, he positioned himself over her, taking her wrists and holding them stretched out above her head.

"It's all right," he whispered. "You can relax. It's all right."

"But it's so hard—"

He entered her in a swift motion, burying himself in her to the hilt. She cried out as she took the full length of him, her body rigid and trembling. Then she relaxed, and with the release of tension, she shivered, causing her hips to involuntarily buck against him.

He drew out almost completely, still holding her, and slowly entered her again, inch by fraction of an inch. He did this again and again and still again, until Julia's head thrashed from side to side, her eyes closed as she focused in on the feelings he was bringing from her. He released her wrists, and she curled around him, gripping him with both arms and legs as he quickened the pace, slamming into her harder and faster with his full, rigid length.

This time when she came it was with such force that she grabbed the bed covers and bit down on them to keep from screaming. Her body thrashed with the spasms, churning against him, bucking and grinding. When she was well into it, Slocum let go and burst inside her, and this she felt. It drove her once more into the chasm, and again she arched in to him. Slocum stayed with her, pounding into her until the sweet agony of her climax had passed and she lay back, spent and exhausted.

He rolled off of her. She tucked herself next to him and stroked the hard muscles of his chest.

"You're going out again. When?"

"Tonight."

"Marshal Reed came by today."

Slocum sat up. "Reed? What the hell did he want?"

"I think he wanted to know what room I was in. You didn't send him?"

"No. I didn't send him."

"Can I stay here? I didn't like him, and it makes me nervous to think he knows where I'm sleeping."

"I don't like him much, either," Slocum said. "You sleep in this bed tonight. We'll have the clerk move you to another room in the morning."

"You're not leaving yet, are you? Could you stay with me just a little longer?"

Slocum leaned over her and smiled. Her eyes were bright and clear, with no hint of the trouble he had seen in them earlier. He bent down and once more began the long, slow body kiss.

14

The Garrison House kept its own stable across the side street to the north, a fine building of sawn slab lumber with a loft above and sturdy stalls of thick pine posts and rails. Slocum's lantern sputtered in the cool night air as he led his horse from the stall and saddled him, tightening the front and back cinch and checking the stirrups and the breast collar. He strapped on the rifle scabbard and slipped the freshly cleaned and oiled Henry into it. The sorrel anticipated the night ride and showed its impatience by pawing at the ground with one front hoof. Its big nostrils were flared and its breath steamed.

He would head back to the ranch where he had killed the man named Hoffman. He needed to be on the ground before daylight, ready when the first stirrings of the day began and the first man, rumpled and bleary-eyed, stumbled out to the privy.

He was uncertain of just how he would end it, but end it was what he meant to do.

He slipped the bit into the horse's mouth and fitted the headstall up over its ears, and he heard riders: the crunch of a shod hoof in gravel, a whisper, a muffled cough outside in the dark. Several men. He heard the creak of saddle leather and the blowing of one horse, then another.

He doused the lantern and moved to the big double doors at the rear of the barn. The doors were open a few inches and he stood there and listened, letting his eyes adjust to the blackness.

Might be a couple of hotel customers coming in, except that it was late and they were approaching from the back, quietly. No need to do that unless you were concerned about being seen on the street.

He heard them pass by the door—four or five riders leading an extra, riderless horse—and continue across the road to the back of the hotel. The horses shuffled to a stop, and there came another creak of saddle leather as one rider swung down, then the ching of spurs as another followed. More light coughing, dry and nervous. He heard the rasp of metal against leather, and the unmistakable ratchet of a lever-action rifle.

Then a voice, softened in an attempt at quiet, but still deep and heavy enough that it carried to Slocum's ears.

"You mind them ponies, boy. We'll be back directly, and likely we'll be hurrying."

Deward Halsey. Behind this came a shrill, nervous burst of laughter, quickly suppressed.

Bobby Todd.

Slocum edged through the big doors and into the inky blackness of the alley. His eyes had accustomed themselves to the dark, and he could make out vague shapes before him: a granite boulder nearly obscured by sagebrush, a pile of garbage, the mound of manure shoveled out from the stalls. Beyond, the occasional light of residences glowed a flickering yellow. He looked toward the rear of the hotel, but not directly at it, knowing that in darkness the edges of vision were sharper. He saw a general sort of movement, the hazy blur of someone's white shirt—fifty yards away, maybe sixty. It was after twelve o'clock, but the night was moonless. The stars provided more decoration than light.

He waited while they moved with grim caution up the alley, four men and at least two of them carrying rifles. They fanned out across the side street so as not to jostle each other and give themselves away with senseless noise. The boy remained behind with the horses.

Bold. Even in darkness. To come right into Garrison, and take her.

Slocum could not follow them without being seen by the horse handler, and to go around the barn and brace them in the street, alone and in the open, would be to get cut down—or to scatter them like Indians. He knew Bobby Todd was among them. He'd heard the laughter, remembered it from when he dangled by his wrists over the blaze of brush and scrub pine. If the fire had done nothing else, it had burned the sound of that laughter into his brain. Slocum wanted this chance. But he would first have to deal with the horse handler.

He moved to the cover of the boulder, and paused there to determine if his movement had been spotted. He saw no nervous scurrying, and in a moment he heard the voice of the handler speaking in soft tones to the horses.

Ahead of Slocum, beyond the rock, was an open stretch of ground, dotted with calf-high sagebrush. He began picking his way toward the horses, planting each foot deliberately, knowing there were dry bits of brush down there that would snap beneath his weight; there was nothing he could do about them. Still he heard the handler's soothing voice.

One of the horses turned its head toward Slocum and whickered.

Slocum had the Navy Colt out of its holster. He froze. His clothing was fairly dark, and his hands were gloved. He moved the pistol behind him so the brass frame would not reflect stray light. If he kept still, there was a chance the handler would not see him, though he was only twenty yards away. If he were spotted, then the ball would open right here. He laid his thumb on the hammer of the Colt, ready to draw it back.

But the handler, whom Slocum now could see, was more concerned with the noise the horse had made, and he whipped up a gloved hand to pinch off the animal's nostrils and prevent it from happening again. Slocum remained stiff and quiet, barely breathing. After an eternity of seconds the handler relaxed, released the horse and set about building himself a smoke.

From the front of the hotel: the sound of booted feet mounting the wooden steps of the porch.

Slocum crept on through the brush, no longer concerned with the noise. The handler was busy with his makings and the distractions from up front, and there was no more time for caution. If Slocum had to kill this one, he would.

A shout came from the hotel porch. The handler struck a match, illuminating a slack, beard-bristled face, deeply shadowed around the eyes. The handler cocked an ear, listening, the twisted cigarette dangling from his bottom lip.

Slocum rushed him from the last ten feet.

One of the horses snorted and danced sideways. The handler turned—perhaps a glint of movement had alerted him as Slocum swung the Colt, chopping down—and he raised his arm, dropping the match and skidding to the right, the pistol barrel bouncing off his shoulder, a blow meant for the side of his angular head. He opened his mouth to shout, and Slocum brought the pistol back around, catching him in the jaw with the barrel end. The man yowled in anger and swung to the left, pivoting, going all the way around, and when he came up again, there was a knife in his hand, a narrow-bladed, nasty little pig-sticker. Slocum saw the stroke coming in and lanced out with a foot and caught the handler just above the knee. The handler grunted in pain but followed through with his swing, and Slocum felt the knife whip through his shirt, the tip barely kissing his skin. He lifted the Navy Colt and fired, the gunshot an eruption of flash and spark, simultaneous with a shot from the front of the hotel.

The muzzle blast lighted the handler's face as the pistol ball took him high on the nose, and then the darkness surged back over him as he fell. Before he hit the ground, Slocum was running up the alley.

At the porch he halted and peered around the edge of the wall. A man he didn't recognize, as thin and blackbird rangy as the man who had just died, stood on the porch with a short-barreled Sheriff's Colt in his hand, pointed skyward. No doubt meant to be a sentry, to stand guard while the rest of them took care of business inside. Light spilled onto the porch from the open lobby doors, and the man found the proceedings in there more interesting than the prospects of someone coming up at him from the street.

Slocum heard Deward's voice, raised and booming.

"She ain't in her regular room. She's moved and you're going to tell us where. Ten seconds, and then me and these fellows break you into little pieces and commence searching every room you got, one by one. You hear? You won't have no paying guests then, we'll run them all into the street."

Slocum stepped out in view of the sentry and raised his pistol. "Hey."

The sentry whirled and spotted him there with the pistol raised and cocked. He dropped his own piece to the boards of the porch, turned and ran.

Someone from inside said, "Where's Luther going?"

The clump of booted feet, and another man rushed out to the porch. It was the one called Jason, the man who had helped Bobby Todd string Slocum up in the tree. Slocum said, once more, "Hey."

Jason fired at Slocum's voice even before he got turned around. He missed by a yard, and Slocum shot him in the chest. Jason's arms came up as he fell, his own pistol flying, and his body made a hollow thud against the porch planks when he landed.

Slocum leaped to the porch and crouched beside the doorway. Deward Halsey's big face was just beyond the desk, and his huge, black-haired hand twisted the shirt of the balding desk clerk. Bobby Todd was across the desk, the register book pulled over to him as if he'd been trying to make heads or tails from the scratchings there.

At sight of Slocum, Deward released the clerk and drew his pistol, in the same movement diving behind the counter. Bobby Todd, already laughing, fired, and turned with the roar still hot in Slocum's ears, to head toward the dining room. A door there would lead to the kitchen and from there to the back of the hotel. Slocum put the sights on him, but Deward's gun barked, taking a chunk from the jamb above Slocum's head. Slocum ducked back from the flying splinters, cursing, then lunged forward once more and fired, putting the bullet through the front desk at about the spot he figured Deward to be.

Deward jumped at the same instant, hit the floor on his shoulder and rolled, with amazing agility for a man of his bulk. As he came up, his gun belched again, fired without aim, the ball whizzing uncomfortably, angrily, above Slocum's head—close enough to make him wince and duck back down. Deward was up and moving, following his brother.

Slocum rushed into the lobby. Mr. Conway appeared on the first landing of the stairwell in his robe and slippers, carrying his own small pistol, an invitation to get killed. Slocum ignored the man's shouted question and hurried through the lobby, pausing at the entrance to the darkened dining room. He could hear the two Halsey brothers crashing through the kitchen. A pot hit the floor with a rattling clang. Slocum followed, his own breath hissing in his ears. As he reached the kitchen, he heard the wrench of wood as one of the Halseys kicked out the back door. He dove on, ducking to the left as another shot ripped the darkness with a spray of red sparks and yellow flame, and then the Halseys were through the door and outside.

Slocum came on. He kept low and reached the fractured doorway.

The horses had moved a little back from the hotel. Bobby Todd was already mounted and riding off, whipping with the reins. Deward was just swinging up, a flurry of movement in the darkness. Slocum fired and saw the horse jerk sideways and then rear, Deward fighting to maintain balance and get aboard at the same time. A blast came from Deward's gun, again without aim but again searingly close, and then Deward was aboard, clinging low to the side of his horse like a Comanche, and the horse was running, the great grunts of its breath audible with each thrust of momentum.

Slocum was certain he'd wounded the horse. Deward would go to ground somewhere close by when the animal gave out, and Slocum was tempted to mount and give chase. But the darkness was a serious impediment. It would be too easy for them to lie in wait and blast him out of the saddle as he pounded by.

He let the hammer down easy on his last round and waited for his breathing to return to normal. His teeth were clenched with twisting force, his entire body as taut as piano wire.

He returned to the lobby. Mr. Conway and the desk clerk were out front, kneeling over Jason's body. Other guests, a half dozen or so of the braver ones, lined the staircase in various stages of undress, curious but not brave enough to venture all the way down.

Conway said, "They came right into town again, as bold as brass! I heard them break into Julia's room, I thought they had her—"

"You heard them, and it took you this long to come down and do something?" Slocum asked.

"They didn't get her. She wasn't in her room. Where is she, Slocum?"

"In my room."

Conway's eyes flared, but before he could say anything, Julia came up behind Slocum. She gasped when she spotted the body, and she grabbed Slocum's arm. She pressed her face against his shoulder.

The desk clerk looked at Slocum. "This one's sure deader than hell. I say good for you, mister."

"There's another one out back." Slocum said. "You might want to run and fetch the Marshal."

15

Marshal Reed wasn't at the faro table in the Gold Slipper, and he wasn't at the office. No one knew where he'd gone or could say when he might be back. Slocum had the bodies dragged over and laid out on the boardwalk in front of the jail, hands crossed in front of them as if in a funeral viewing, where Reed would have no trouble finding them when he showed up.

Slocum spent the remainder of the night on a chair outside Julia's door, his pistol freshly loaded and on his lap. He could hear her crying, and the temptation to go in and comfort her was great, but he knew where things would wind up if he did. Now was not the time.

Mr. Conway had retreated to his own room. Hiding from it. He had spoken no more than a dozen words to Slocum since the ruckus. He looked dazed.

No one came. When morning arrived, Slocum stood and stretched, went downstairs for a pot of coffee, brought it and two mugs to Julia's room and knocked on the door, calling to her so that she would know it was him. Her voice, when she told him to enter, was thin and distant. She sat up in bed, her eyes red against the paleness of her skin. She wore a white cotton night-gown and nothing else. She reached for him.

Instead of coming to her, he gave her a mug of coffee, and filled one for himself. His eyes burned, and his throat was raw from the endless cigarettes he'd smoked while on watch.

"When you're ready," he told her, "get yourself presentable, and we'll go."

She cradled her coffee cup in both hands and looked up at him. "Go where?"

"I'm moving you. Someplace safe."

He thought she'd fight him, refuse to be moved, citing some nonsense about how she wanted to be near him while he fought for her; and when she only nodded and lowered her head, he felt a flash of worry. The fight last night had shaken her, though she had seen none of it, only the dead man on the porch. But she had heard the gunfire and the noise, smelled the powder smoke and knew that they had been here—*here*—after her, and had Slocum left town an hour earlier, they would have gotten her.

He waited in the hall while she dressed. As he finished a second cup of coffee, Mr. Conway came out of his room buttoning his vest. He stopped and gave Slocum a haunted look.

"Everything well?"

Slocum saw the deterioration in the man's face. He might be a presence in the big city, strolling through marble hallways carrying with him some sort of financial power that made lesser beings tremble before him like leaves in a breeze, but in the face of violent and sudden, acrid-smelling death he was like any other man— small and afraid.

"I'm moving her. Today."

"Where?"

"Best you don't know."

"I'm her father, for God's sake."

Slocum nodded. "Yes, and they come take you and put the boots to you, you might still be her father, but you'll be the man to tell them where she is. Right before they kill you."

"They wouldn't get it out of me," Conway said, indignant, defiant. Slocum remembered him on the stairs with the little pistol. Wary and much too late, as if his arrival was more posturing than anything else.

"You think on it, real hard," Slocum said. "You want to take the chance?"

For a moment they faced each other. Slocum watched Conway's resolve crumble, as the truth seeped into him. The man sagged and his gaze dropped.

"Of course you're right," Conway said. "We all hope that we're made of sterner stuff. But in the end we are what we are."

Dr. Reddick was hesitant at first, but only because he felt the town would frown upon Julia and do her reputation damage if it came to light: a young lady alone in the home of a single man.

"We're not talking about propriety, Doctor," Slocum said. "We're talking about survival."

Reddick blinked as he considered this. "Maybe you had better tell me just what it is these people want to do."

Slocum told him.

Reddick flushed, hearing such things with Julia right there in the room. He shook his head, disbelieving. "I knew they were little better than savages, but I had no idea they'd go this far. Of course, she's more than welcome. I'll fix up the back room."

He hurried off to take care of it, leaving Slocum and Julia alone in the examining room. She stood with her satchel of clothes on the floor next to her feet. Her hands were folded in front of her, and she held herself erect, as if defying her fear.

"How long?" she asked.

"Not long, I think. Stay inside and out of sight. Don't give the doctor any more trouble than we're already giving him."

"I'm not an idiot!" she snapped. Then she looked pained at having allowed the tension to get to her, and she came to him. He held her for a moment and then stepped back.

"How can you turn it off like that?" she asked. "How can you be so cold?"

"There's a time for it, Julia. This is the time for something else."

Reddick came back, and Slocum faced him. "Do you have a gun?"

"Yes, I have one. It's old, but it still shoots."

"Get it."

Reddick went to the bottom drawer of his rolltop desk and brought out a huge and ancient Walker Colt. He handed it to Slocum, who inspected it. It was capped and loaded.

Slocum gave it back to him. "Keep it close, and anybody comes poking around, make certain they know you've got it. Can you use it?"

"I've lived in this country for fifteen years. I have to know how to use it. Do you think they'll show up here?"

"It's hard to say what they'll do. They want her bad enough, they might take the whole town apart, piece by piece. I plan to stop them before they get that far, but if they kill me I'd like to know that they'll meet with a last line of defense."

"They'll have to kill me to get her," Reddick said, and looked at Julia. It was a long, lingering look, taking in every angle and curve of her body. Julia looked back at him and then away.

"Doctor," Slocum said, "if they find out she's here, they will kill you."

The man at the livery stable was waiting when Slocum came in to get his horse. He was a spare, wiry little gent with sharp features.

"What is it?" Slocum asked.

The man fidgeted. He refused to look Slocum in the eyes. "Marshal Reed was here, looking for you. Needs to see you real bad."

"About those men last night? Did he happen to mention just where the hell he was while all that shooting was going on?"

"Mister, I guess if he'd wanted me to know that he'd've told me. All he said was he wants to see you."

Slocum had no more regard for Marshal Reed than he had for a coyote, but it might be that the man had information that would help—if he was inclined to part with it. Slocum could not pass up the chance.

He directed the liveryman to saddle his horse for him, and left the stables. As he made his way along the plank sidewalk, he admitted to himself that he was as anxious to throw last night's killings into Reed's lean face as he was anything else—*here, see what it's come to*? The man had been so busy strutting and combing his hair, and killing mule skinners by example. Perhaps now he'd see it was time to climb down off the pedestal and take a hand. He could claim no lack of jurisdiction now. The fight had been brought to him.

The Marshal's office and jail were two doors down from the Gold Slipper, convenient to the faro tables. Slocum opened the door and entered. A large, scarred desk filled the corner of the room, and Reed was seated behind it with his hat on. He regarded Slocum with a blank expression, and when Slocum turned to close the door, Reed brought up a double-barreled greener from behind the desk and trained it on Slocum's middle.

Slocum froze, staring at the twin muzzles, two black and sightless eyes.

"So that's the way of it," he said.

"You will remove the hardware. Carefully."

Slocum unbuckled his gunbelt and lowered it to the floor, then nudged it toward the desk with the toe of his boot. "What are you? Cousin? Second cousin? Nephew?"

"Jason Hodges and Wilson Halsey."

"Who are they?"

"That's them two boys you busted last night and laid out on my doorstep. I am a City Marshal, Slocum, and I have just treed myself a murderer. You just get yourself along through this doorway to where them cells are." He smirked, his cold eyes sparking. "You give me a reason, I'll kill you. Doesn't even have to be a big reason."

"You hit me with both those barrels it'll make a hell of a mess."

"I guess I'd manage to clean it up."

Slocum backed through the rear door into the cell

area. There were three cells, iron bars set in thick mortar, all stone-floored so they could be washed out easily. The cells were empty, and the door to the nearest one stood open, waiting for him. Slocum fought the urge to bolt, knowing it was all Reed would need to unload on him. At this range the shotgun would literally blow him in two. Reed poked him with it, directing him inside.

He slammed the door behind Slocum. The bars were set solid and did not rattle; there was only the cold, hard clink as the lock plate met the iron frame, and then the jingle of keys as Reed locked him in.

Slocum said, "You must be blood to them somehow."

Reed smiled at him. "You don't know shit, boy. You were warned, and you didn't pay attention. You'll have to take what you got coming."

"And what's that?"

"You'll see when it happens. Until then you ain't going nowhere."

The cell was six feet by six feet, not even wide enough for Slocum to stretch his arms out. There was a slop bucket and a pallet of dirty blankets on the floor. No room to pace, had he been inclined to do so, which he was not. The War had taught him patience, laid out on a hill with a rifle, for hours, waiting for the chance to put a bullet into a Union officer at four or five hundred yards, the sweat rolling down his face and into his eyes, insects buzzing around him. The years since had only added to that sureness. He sat now, legs crossed, in the corner, staring through the bars at nothing, seeing everything, waiting, gathering his strength for whatever might be coming.

The morning passed and merged into afternoon. The sunlight shifted and poured in through the tiny window behind him, sending his shadow long out onto the floor beyond the cell. The sunlight dwindled to twilight.

A towheaded boy in a battered straw hat brought him a bucket of stew, and he ate. He stood up after and stretched, used the slop bucket and then settled into the corner once more. He dozed a little.

It was well past dark when he heard men in the outer office. There was the rumble of voices, but he could not make them out, or put faces to them. He tensed, waiting. He would not lay plans; you had to wait and see what chances were presented to you, and then act upon them. You could not anticipate anything.

The office doorknob turned, and Reed entered with a lantern. Behind him came two men, and Slocum recognized Deward Halsey by his massive build and the smell of wood smoke and sweat he carried with him, filling the room with his presence. His steps were solid and sure, weighted so that the man was in balance and square at all times.

Reed placed the lantern on a shelf and turned up the wick. The third man was lean and sinewy, about forty, with hollowed temples and thick, dark eyebrows.

"Awake, Slocum?" Reed said.

Slocum got to his feet, his hands hanging loose at his sides.

"He's awake and he'd best enjoy it while he can," the lean man said. "He ain't going to stay awake much longer." He stepped forward and spat through the bars. Slocum felt the slime strike his cheek and slide down toward his chin. He looked at the man and did not wipe it away.

"You're dead, you son of a bitch," the lean man said. "You hear me? All that's left is to bury you."

Deward grabbed the man's arm and pulled him back. He looked Slocum once over, up and down, his face expressionless. He glanced at Reed.

"You done good, boy. We'll take it from here." He turned back to Slocum. "Last time I seen you, mister, I give you a warning. It was sincere and heartfelt, but you decided you didn't have to pay it no mind. You ain't going to get off just being marked this time. This time it's the whole shitteree."

"I say we lay him out here and now," the lean man said. He unsheathed his pistol.

"You stand easy, boy!" Deward barked. He grinned at Slocum. "Harlan here is a little upset. That was his baby brother whose ticket you punched on that porch last night."

"He had it coming," Slocum said.

Deward nodded. "Maybe so. Now it's your turn to take what you got coming. After you tell us where you hid the girl."

Slocum said nothing.

"You're going to tell us sooner or later, boy. You might as well get to it."

"He ain't going to tell you nothing," Reed said. "I know his type. He'll stand there like a rock for hours, just to spite us."

"He don't have hours," Deward said. "He don't get but about two minutes, starting now, and then I commence to putting bullets in him. You hear me, Slocum? I'm going to start with both your knees, then work my way up. You'll beg me to kill you before I'm through."

Reed said, "Not here, Deward."

Deward whirled to glare, and Reed took a step back, as if expecting a fist. Deward said, "What do you mean, not here? You don't boss me, Reed. You know better than that."

"Think about it," Reed said. "There's been too much shooting in town already. The people are going to get fed up, especially if I take a man in and he gets shot dead in his cell. You want me to stay on here as Marshal and do you any good, you best listen to me. You'll have people poking around here you'd rather not see."

"Maybe you got a better way to do it," Deward said, biting off the words.

"He ain't going to tell you nothing, I'll guarantee it. Take him out somewhere and put a bullet in him. We'll say he escaped, and when we tracked him down he put up a fight. I'll find out where the girl is, after."

Deward studied him for a moment, considering it. "We'd better find her, Reed. If that old man dies because we didn't get this done, Slocum here ain't the only one I'm holding responsible. You hear?"

"I hear."

Slocum said, "You can't really set store by what that old woman tells you. She's a witch doctor. She knows nothing about real medicine."

Deward stabbed a blunt finger at Slocum. "You listen. That old woman helped birth most of us, and told beforehand whether we'd come out he or she, and never was she wrong. She's patched our breaks and mended our cuts and nursed us through fevers and plugged our bullet holes. She's said when the hard rains was coming, and the big snows, and she's told us when there weren't going to be no rains. And she's always been right. I don't care if she sees it in the guts of a chicken or in coffee grounds or where she sees it, but she's always dead center. Am I lying, Harlan?"

"Nossir," Harlan said. "It's the bald truth."

"If she tells me the sky is going to turn yellow and rain iron balls tomorrow, then I'm heading for cover. She said there'd be a woman come along with a streak of white in her hair, and she'd be the one to save him. And I ride up to that camp a few days ago and there she is. That old girl knows, Slocum. She *knows*."

"Your father's dying," Slocum said. "There is no girl who can climb into bed with him and save him."

"Reed," Deward said without looking around, "you take this man out in the sagebrush somewhere and put a bullet through his head. Then leave him out there for the varmints."

"I thought I was going to find the girl."

"I'll find the girl myself. You're the Marshal and so concerned about looking bad, if I let you do it you'll take forever. I'm going back to the house and check on the old man, then I'm fetching Bobby Todd and we're going to take this town apart." He turned then and looked at Reed. "You figure you can handle this cracker?"

Reed stiffened. "I can handle him."

"Run fetch the horses, Harlan."

Harlan left the room. Reed unlocked the cell door while Deward covered Slocum with his pistol, the black Remington looking small and light in his massive fist. Reed bound Slocum's hands behind him with a length of cotton cord, jerking the knots hard; then the three of them moved through the office to a back door, which opened onto the alley. They stood waiting, Deward's pistol barrel digging into Slocum's back, until they heard horses.

"It's Harlan," Reed said. "He's fast."

"He's eager," Deward said. "He's going with you. He wants to see this man die, and right quick."

"I don't need no help," Reed said.

"He's going. Where you taking him to do it?"

Reed stepped into the alley. Slocum could sense the man's irritation. Harlan rode up leading two horses, one of which was Slocum's. He tossed the reins to Reed.

"You don't have to know everything, do you, Deward?"

Deward chuckled, a dark, rumbling sound. "No, boy, I don't. But I do want to know when it's done."

"You'll know. I'll come tell you."

Together Harlan and Reed assisted Slocum onto the back of his horse.

Slocum did not fight them, conserving his strength for the ride out of town and whatever came after. Sitting upright, he might have a chance; if he fought them and they tied him facedown across the saddle, he would have no chance at all.

Reed mounted his own horse. He reined around, saying nothing else to Deward, and the three of them started down the alley at a walk, headed for the edge of town. There was no moon.

16

They angled south and west, through the scattering of board and batten shacks marking the edge of town. They rode slowly without speaking, Reed and Harlan not wishing to draw more attention than was necessary. Some of the shacks were occupied, leaking lamplight, but most were dark.

When they were at last out onto open country, Harlan loosened up and started badgering Reed.

"You should have kilt this boy earlier, Reed, first you had the chance. Then maybe Jason would be still up and kicking, 'stead of laid flat out on a slab."

"Shut up," Reed said.

"Deward's right. You ain't never had no sense and never will. Now my brother's dead. Don't seem fair."

"Shut the hell up," Reed said. "You behave, when the time comes I'll let you pull the trigger."

"You'll be lucky I don't pull it on you after."

Slocum half-listened, working his wrists against the ropes. There was little give in the cotton cords, and the night air was causing his shoulders to stiffen up.

Once, when they had gone a few hundred yards from town, Harlan reined in. "Here's good enough."

Reed kept going, jerking Slocum's horse along with him. "No. I don't want him found anywhere near town, and I don't want them hearing the shot."

"Deward wants him dead, and damned fast," Harlan whined.

"To hell with what Deward wants."

They occupied themselves in argument for the next hour, a nipping sort of quarrel that sounded well worn and familiar. Reed, Slocum thought, must be the family whipping boy.

He worked at the ropes.

The dark and rounded shapes of sagebrush faded on either side of them into the larger darkness beyond. The edges of the foothills loomed before them. They crossed a creek, down a steep cutbank and then up the other side, the water barely over the horses' fetlocks. Slocum controlled his balance with his feet in the stirrups.

Into the foothills, sage giving way to rock and scrub pine, starlight shining against granite. The small creeks became more common. This was strange country to Slocum, well south of the Halseys' territory—out here, his dead body when found might somehow not be connected with them. Reed seemed determined to travel as far from town as possible to do the job. Probably a display of rebelliousness, Slocum reasoned—an attempt to say that in this, at least, he still had control, no matter what Deward wanted.

After two hours they pulled up at the mouth of a narrow draw. There had been the sound of crickets, but the noise of the horses silenced them. The three men sat their mounts for a moment, saying nothing, only breathing. One of the horses blew. After a minute the crickets started up again.

"I wonder if we should maybe just bury him," Reed said.

"Bury him?" Harlan smirked. "We didn't bring no damn shovel. Anyways, you said you was going to make it look like he broke out and give you a fight."

"I'll do it however I want to do it!" Reed snarled. He drew a pistol from his sash.

"No," Harlan said, pulling his own revolver. "Let me pop him."

Slocum slammed spurs into his horse's belly. Its grunt of surprise as it lunged forward was as loud as Harlan's sharp cry—"Hey, *shit*!"—as the horse plowed into Reed's mount. Reed's pistol went off into the air, and the other two horses dodged sideways. Slocum's horse was out and running, up and across the slope, Slocum low over the pommel, feeling the saddle horn punch him below the breastbone, hearing the shot in the same instant as the horse beneath him gave another grunt of surprise, faltered, then plunged on.

Hit. The damn thing had been hit.

It carried him a hundred yards farther before stumbling again. It halted, quivering, a strange, heavy groan shaking it from deep inside. It went down. Slocum stepped from the saddle as it collapsed, and the animal was dead even before he got clear of it.

He had no time to cuss the loss, for now he was afoot, alone in dark and unfamiliar country.

He heard the hiss of water ahead. He ran toward the sound, clumsily, with his hands still cinched behind his back, his long-heeled riding boots slipping on loose stones. Up and across the next ridge, keeping low and ducking over the edge close to the trunk of a tall pine to keep from being skylined and inviting a bullet. He heard Reed and Harlan's horses thumping through the brush behind him. He kept going, the slope beneath him turning sharp and steep, the rush of water louder now. A creek would mean willows, and he hoped they'd be thick enough to hide a man.

They were. The roar at the head of the canyon was fierce and probably meant a waterfall, but lower down, where the creek leveled out and widened, the willows grew thick and wet and higher than his head. He plunged into them, the branches whipping at his face and neck. Far into them, he stopped. He strained to hear above the ragged pant of his own breath.

Nothing but the hiss of the creek. Reed and Harlan had not yet crossed the divide, and with any luck it would be a few minutes before they figured out where he'd gone. He squatted down and stepped backward through his bound arms, got his hands in front of his face and went to work on the ropes with his teeth.

There were several knots, but after he had worked the second one loose, the cords eased up enough that he could work his wrists free, peel the loops off and hurl them from him. He rubbed his wrists, listening for the sounds of horses, voices. Hearing none, he crept forward through the willows toward the noise of the waterfall. He needed to see what sort of box he was in.

The canyon narrowed a dozen yards ahead, the soil giving way to barren rock, blunt and ungiving and slick with moisture. Another twenty yards brought him to the falls themselves, a roaring cascade of water twenty feet straight up and down, the white mist showing plain in the moonless starlight.

No way out here. He was bottled up, cornered like an animal.

He worked his way back down to the willows, and he heard them at the mouth of the canyon, first their horses and the squeak of saddle leather, then their voices, calling to each other.

"Work a cross pattern from here on up," Reed hollered.

"I know what the hell to do!" Harlan growled.

Slocum ducked into the willows, his lips involuntarily pulled back from his teeth. He waited as they worked their way slowly and methodically toward him, crisscrossing back and forth between the steep ridges on either side, plunging their horses in and back out of the creek.

"Slocum!" Harlan shouted. "You're dead already! Might just as well come out and lay down!"

Slocum waited. Coiled, ready.

When one of them reached him, he would make a fight. It might not last long, perhaps only seconds before the other one rode up and finished him, but it would be a fight, and he would take at least one of them down with him.

He heard them crashing closer, near the edge of the willows.

"He may have snuck back over the ridge," Reed said.

"He's in here," Harlan said. "I can smell him."

Reed moved his horse on past the edge of the thicket, heading for the north side of the creek. Harlan remained where he was, facing the willows; Slocum could almost see him craned forward in the saddle, attempting to pierce the darkness through sheer willpower. Slocum imagined the man's nostrils twitching, trying to sniff him out.

"Bastard," Harlan hissed, barely above a whisper. Then, louder, "You in there, Slocum? When you run, you better run hard. I'm going to blow a hole through you."

He nudged his horse forward. The animal did not care for the dense willows. It tossed its head and tried to sidle away.

Slocum tensed.

Harlan spurred savagely, and the horse gave a final squeal and lunged into the thicket.

Slocum unwound like a spring, shot forward, grabbed Harlan by the shirt and yanked him out of the saddle.

Harlan shouted Reed's name as he fell. His pistol went off when he landed, the blast scorching the air inches from Slocum's face. Slocum slammed a fist into Harlan's midsection, but he was off-balance and the blow was only half-strength. Harlan doubled up and tried to roll away. Slocum grabbed him by the hair and felt the gun barrel slam into his own shoulder. He reached for Harlan's bony wrist, caught it, slammed it hard against the ground. And again. Harlan choked with rage.

"*Reed!*" he screamed.

Slocum heard Reed's horse coming toward them. He felt the vibrations through the ground and heard the splash as Reed crossed the creek. Harlan's left fist came up against his ear, jolting him, stinging. Slocum hurtled in with a right that glanced off the side of Harlan's head, and then the two of them were groping, rolling on the ground, each grasping for the advantage that would lead to the kill. Harlan scratched and kicked, his breath wheezing from his open mouth.

"*Harlan!*" Reed called, panic in his voice. "*Where are you?*"

Harlan shouted, a hoarse, wordless cry. Reed answered, and Slocum heard him change direction and gallop toward them. Harlan's hands were at Slocum's throat, thumbs digging in. He was making a noise that was both whining and eager. Slocum sent a knee into his belly, but the man hung on. Slocum found Harlan's jaw and pushed, bending Harlan's head back on his neck. Harlan's voice took on a new strain, the anger graveling his throat. He tried to keep his hold on Slocum's neck, but he was at the end of his reach. He thrashed.

Slocum felt something hard and angular below his leg. Harlan's pistol. Reed was still coming, closer now, almost here but slowed up as his horse fought against entering the willows. Slocum gave Harlan a final shove, rolled away and found the pistol, grabbing it around the cylinder. He got to his knees and swung as Harlan lunged for him.

The pistol grips caught Harlan just above the ear, making a hollow sound. Harlan dodged sideways, drunkenly, arms flailing. Slocum swung the pistol again, more savage and deliberate this time, and felt the skull beneath crack and give way, the sound from Harlan's mouth no longer angry, but the limp cry of a wounded wolf as it goes down. Slocum came down on him one last time, with all his strength behind it, and felt the warm blood spatter his face. He upended the gun, thumbing back the hammer, rose and turned just as Reed's horse plunged into the thicket nearly on top of him.

Slocum jumped back and fired, the blast lighting up the darkness, showing the flared nostrils of the spooked horse, its eyes wide and crazed, and beyond it Reed's wild face. The horse wheeled, heedless of the bit, and struck Slocum on the shoulder as it thundered around. As Slocum fell, he fired once more, the shot going wide. One more bullet wasted. The willows caught him, and as he struggled for balance he waited for Reed to fire back and blast him into nothingness; but Reed was putting the spurs to his horse, as fully spooked himself as the animal under him, wanting only to get gone, out of there, away from Slocum and the willows and death.

Slocum wasted no more shots. He heard Reed gallop from the canyon, the hoofbeats fading until the only sounds there with him were the hiss of the creek and the soft soughing of the night breezes through the pines.

Harlan was stone dead, his skull crushed. Slocum knelt and rummaged for the pistol belt that held the holster and the canvas bag containing balls and powder and caps. He reloaded the pistol in the blackness next to the body, working by feel.

He rose, strapped the belt on and stuffed the pistol into the holster. He set off, up over the ridge. He would come down the canyon they had first entered—and he would go cautiously, even though he knew Reed would not be waiting for him. The man would flog it into town as fast as he could.

Ten miles, more or less. He judged it to be three hours or so before dawn. A long walk ahead of him, and Harlan's horse was nowhere in sight.

17

The dawn came, cold and gray, before he reached town, and the dew settled on the back of his neck and dampened his shirt. The wet sage slapped at his legs and drenched his pants to the knees.

He hurried on, faster now as the sky lightened and the first sight of Garrison came to him, and with the sight the early morning smells of wood smoke and coffee.

He had to get there. Now.

His feet were raw inside his boots. The deep churning of dread in his gut wanted to turn to panic. He veered west of the main street and came in over a rise behind Dr. Reddick's house, not wanting to approach it from the front. At the crest of the rise he stopped.

A crowd of people, not many, perhaps a dozen. They milled around in the street in front of Reddick's place in various stages of dress, men in coats but no collars, no shirts, boots yanked hurriedly on, even one man still in a nightdress. The women were all bundled, but sleep was still in their hair and on their faces, along with the blank, numb look of shock.

Slocum sagged, and felt something go out of him.

There was a body in the yard.

People stood around it, talking, looking down at it. Presently a man came out of the house with a blanket and covered it.

They had come. Somehow, Deward had found out where Slocum had hidden Julia, and he had come and taken her, and when Dr. Reddick made a fight, Deward or Bobby Todd or one of the others had shot him down in sight of his own front door.

Slocum came down the hill, all speed gone from him now. The people heard him coming and turned to look. A figure broke from the group and hurried toward him: Mr. Conway in a nightshirt and pants and overcoat, his ridiculous bowler hat yanked down on his head.

"Slocum!" he bellowed. "She's gone! This is where you put her, this is your safe place, and now they've got her!"

Slocum pushed past him without answering, went to the body and pulled the blanket aside.

Dr. Reddick stared at him with eyes that were open and dead. The hole in his forehead was black and bloodless, ringed at the edges with powder burns. Whoever had killed him had held the gun inches away from the man's head, perhaps leaning down from a horse, and blasted his life out.

The Walker Colt was beside him, three of the percussion caps fired. He had gotten off a few defiant rounds, but there were no answering bodies present, nobody but Reddick dead in his yard. Slocum imagined them riding around him in circles, taunting him, like Indians. The ground had been torn up pretty bad.

"Where is she, Slocum?" Conway whined. "Where is my daughter? That great, bearded animal of a man has her now. He's probably already ruined her!"

Slocum stood and faced him, hands clenching and unclenching at his sides. He had nothing he could say to the man, nothing proper or useful.

A woman, coarse and heavy, her hair hurriedly put up and covered with a green scarf, said, "The men didn't take nobody from here. They just shot the doctor and left."

Conway turned and glared at her. "What are you saying, woman? They took my little girl, for God's sake—"

"Shut up, Conway," Slocum said. He looked at the woman. "Did you see it, ma'am?"

The woman nodded. She wore a thick, faded coat, and hugged herself against the sharp morning air. "His daughter's gone all right, but them men never got her. A girl come and took her away before."

"What girl?"

She shrugged. "I didn't know her. Young. Light-colored hair."

"When? How long ago?"

They listened while she told it, how she lived just across the road and had been awake at first light, to punch up the fire and get coffee on for her husband and start the day moving, and how she looked across and saw the blond girl come to the doctor's side door and pound on it as if to stove it in. She saw the doctor come and the two of them speak to each other, the talk getting heated right away, the doctor raising his voice at the girl. He had a gun with him, the same one there on the ground, the big Walker. Pretty quick the dark-haired woman came and joined in the talk, then grabbed a shawl, and the two women left up the alley in the lightening dawn.

Wasn't five minutes later the men came, four of them on horses: big Deward and chinless Bobby Todd and a couple of others the woman hadn't recognized; rode their horses right smack into the yard and Bobby Todd riding his clean up on the porch itself. She'd heard the shots from Dr. Reddick's big gun, twice, then one of the men went in and got him and drug the doctor out, him cussing and fighting them, and he fired one more time, at Deward, the ball coming close enough to burn him, for Deward slapped his hand at the side of his neck like he'd been stung. Then Bobby Todd leaned down from the saddle and shot Dr. Reddick through the head.

Slocum said, "How long?"

"Maybe half an hour since they left. They went all through the house first, I guess looking for that dark-haired girl. I sent my husband to fetch Marshal Reed, but he couldn't find him. Before he got back they was gone."

Conway said, "Slocum, who was this blond girl? Do you know her?"

"Their half sister."

"Then they do have her!"

"Not yet. She's got no love for her brothers. She must have heard what they were planning and come to stop it. I think I know where she'd have taken Julia."

"Then you have to go and get her!"

The woman said, "Mister, excuse me for saying it, but you don't look like you're ready to go nowhere. You're about used up."

Slocum nodded and thanked her for her concern. He addressed the rest of the loiterers, asking for the loan of a horse and a rifle. The thick woman in the scarf spoke

up again, and said that her husband had both, and she
rousted him from the crowd to fetch them.

A few minutes later the man returned leading a
compact bay mare that had four good legs under her,
a surprising horse to belong to a town man. The rifle
he handed Slocum was a Henry repeater, much like
Slocum's own. Along with it came a leather pouch full
of cartridges.

"Mister, how long's it been since you ate?"

"No time. I'll be fine."

"Always time to eat," the man said. "Even if you do it
in the saddle. You hold on. I'll be right back."

The man went off and returned presently with a can-
teen full of coffee and a bag of cold steak and biscuits.
Slocum thanked him.

Conway said, "Find her, Slocum. Find her and I'll
pay you—"

Slocum grabbed Conway by the nightshirt and jerked him forward. He shook him once, hard enough to rattle the man's teeth. "You try to wave your money at me
one more time, mister, and I'm going to break you in
half."

Conway patted the air with his hands, as if to shove
Slocum away. "I'm sorry, I'm just distraught. I don't
know what to do. I'd ride with you, Slocum—"

"No, you wouldn't," Slocum said. "It's your own
daughter, but you still wouldn't ride after her, because
you don't have the stomach for it. Even if you did, I
wouldn't have time to fool with you."

The tracks of the Halseys' horses led north up the main
road. Slocum veered off and headed across country
directly into the foothills. He did not want to lock
horns with them until he was ready, and could choose

the time and place, and right now he had to cover ground in a hurry. If Deward figured out Lorine had come and taken Julia, it would be only a matter of time before they found her, and Slocum suspected they would know where to look, just as he did.

Mid-morning he tethered the mare a quarter mile down the wash from Lorine's brush shelter. He proceeded the rest of the way on foot, carrying the Henry. The wash was narrow and choked with dried weeds, and he crept carefully forward, trying to keep his approach as silent as possible, choosing each step, his eyes and ears alert for any movement or sound, any indication that Deward and his boys had beat him there and were nearby. He flushed a covey of quail, and waited two minutes before he moved again, in case the birds had alerted anyone.

He remembered where the shelter was, but it was so well concealed against the bank that he still almost missed it. He could not risk a shout to announce his approach.

A rifle barrel poked out through the doorway. Slocum ducked down behind a patch of rabbit brush.

"Show yourself again, slow, arms high, or I'm shooting right through those weeds!"

Lorine's voice, high and tight with anxiety.

"Lorine, it's me. Stand easy with that rifle."

"John? John!"

She burst from the shelter and ran toward him, the rifle left behind her. Slocum stood to meet her, and she rushed into his arms and clung to him. She gave a moan of relief and buried her face against his chest.

"Oh, Lordy, I thought they'd killed you dead for sure, John Slocum. I heard Deward talking how Lacklin and Harlan took you out in the hills. I thought you were gone. I got that woman here and didn't know what else to do."

He shushed her, stroking her hair. "You did just fine."

"I was so scared."

"We got to get hidden, someplace safer. They'll come looking."

"They don't know about this place. I never told nobody but you."

She might have told no one, but he did not believe Deward had looked for her very hard. The idea of anyone having a shelter in this area and Deward being unaware of it did not ring true. Deward would know every bird's nest and squirrel hole and bear's den on this mountain, and all it would take for him to come helling in here would be the realization that Lorine was gone and had heard them talking.

There came rustling from the shelter, and he looked up to see Julia emerge and stand there, staring at the two of them. Her hair was loose and windblown and hung to her shoulders, the white streak in the center even more prominent in the fullness. Her face was blank and pale. He headed for her, pulling Lorine along with him.

"You all right?"

She nodded once. "You know this girl, I see."

"Get back inside, Julia. We make a hell of a target, the three of us. You can be angry later."

She flushed, her eyes sparking, then turned and ducked back into the shelter. Lorine followed her, then Slocum, crouching low to clear the top of the crude doorway. Julia sat Indian fashion in the far corner, her dress smoothed tightly over her knees and her hands churning against each other in her lap. She would not look him in the face.

Lorine tried to come to him again, wanting to hold him and be held. Slocum gently pushed her back, smiling at her, and took one of her hands and squeezed it.

"Talk to me, girl. What way did you come in here?"

"I came the regular way I always do. I brung her on the horse and stripped his bridle off and slapped him home so nobody'd see him tied up outside."

Slocum grunted his annoyance. If Deward had not known before where this place was, all he'd have to do was follow the tracks of Lorine's horse. "You heard them talking. About Reed and Harlan."

"Yes."

"You were right in the room with them? They saw you?"

Lorine nodded. "Deward made me fix them a late supper. I was right there. I heard Deward tell Bobby Todd how he figured he knew where this woman was, at the doctor's house, because he watched her daddy and seen him sneak in there. So I—"

"Wait," Slocum said. He looked at Julia. "Your father came there? How did he know where you were?"

She still refused to look at him. He grabbed her chin with thumb and forefinger and turned her face to him. She pulled away.

"I had to go back to my room and get some things," she said. "I saw Dad, and I told him."

"You *told* him?"

"Later he brought money to Dr. Reddick, to try and pay him something for letting me stay there—"

"It got him killed, Julia. Dr. Reddick is dead in his front yard. Bobby Todd shot him the same way he shot your cousin."

She made a pained sound. Her eyes filled and she looked down, one white knuckle going to her lips. "Oh, God," she breathed. "I never thought . . . I didn't mean for him to die, I never meant to—"

Slocum shushed her, not wanting to listen to it. He

was suddenly exhausted. He'd had little sleep for three days and felt stretched to his limits, but he couldn't let his guard down yet. He had to get these women out of here, preferably back to town, but he was unsure of how to go about it.

Lorine looked up, eyes focused on something far away. "They're coming. John, they're coming."

In a moment Slocum heard it as well—the distant crashing of horses moving through brush, coming down the wash toward them. They were here, no later than Slocum could have expected, but much sooner than he would have liked.

The three of them could retreat back down the narrow canyon, but if Deward was as smart as Slocum figured him to be, he'd have men coming from that direction as well, working their way along, hoping to catch them in the middle.

Someone shouted, a quarter mile away. And then came an answering shout, wordless at this distance, but still too close.

Slocum picked up his rifle. "Come, ladies. We need a safer place."

"Mother Agnes's house," Lorine said.

Slocum paused, squinting while he remapped the terrain in his head. He looked at the bank of the wash visible through the doorway. Over that rise, maybe an eighth of a mile or so. He nodded.

"You wait here while I step out and have a look."

He ducked through the doorway and moved out into the sun-drenched dust of the wash, the Henry cocked and ready in his hands. He looked north and south along the cut. Up ahead the draw made a bend, empty now, but the sounds of Deward's approach was much louder, more immediate.

"All right," he hissed, "let's go, and be quick!"

Julia and Lorine emerged, and he herded them
ahead, across the floor of the wash and up the brush-
covered bank on the opposite side, the women moving
swiftly with their skirts gathered high in their hands,
bare legs flashing in the morning sunlight. Slocum
hung back to cover them as they cleared the crest and
started down. He followed after a moment, and was
nearly to the top when the first rider appeared around
the turn and reined up, shouting, whipping a rifle from
his saddle scabbard. He was a man Slocum did not
recognize. His bullet burned the air across Slocum's
legs and scattered rock fifteen feet beyond him.

Slocum dove over the crest and hit the downslope on
his shoulder, tucked and rolled with the Henry across
his chest, made it back to his feet and ran.

A stand of ragged timber beckoned ahead, thick with
deadfalls that would make tough traveling for men on
horseback. They headed for it.

A shout, behind. Another bullet split the air above
them. Slocum turned, knowing he had no choice now.
He dropped to one knee as the rider plunged downslope
with rifle held high for balance. No telling how many
were behind him, but this one was enough. He trained
the Henry on the man, led him for a few yards, and
fired. The bullet took the rider cleanly from his saddle
and toppled him over the back of his horse. Slocum did
not wait around to see him drop.

The women were already among the trees. He
plunged in behind them. Up ahead, Lorine turned
and pointed toward the southeast, indicating that they
should head in that direction. Slocum nodded.

He had his bearings now. Beyond the timber should
be the chicken-infested yard of the herb mixer Lorine
called Mother Agnes.

18

The three of them entered the yard from the trees, scattering the brainless chickens ahead of them.

"Get around the side of the house!" Slocum said. "Don't go across the doorway!"

Mother Agnes's face appeared at the door, her expression startled and curious, and then the rheumy old eyes widened in surprise and anger when she saw Slocum coming with the rifle. She tried to slam the door on him, but he kicked it open before she could get it latched, and he stepped through, rifle cocked and ready.

The inside of the cabin was cluttered with jars full of dried herbs and earthen pots stained with years of use. There was a table and chairs and a stove, and a huge stone fireplace. No men, no guns. The old woman was alone.

He hollered the all clear and stepped outside to cover Lorine and Julia as they hurried past him and in, and then he returned and closed the door behind them.

Mother Agnes faced them, stooped and yet defiant, one gnarled hand supporting herself against the big table.

"Devil man," she croaked at him. "Leave this place."

He ignored her, examining the cabin for means of defense. The windows were curtained and without glass, one on either side of the doorway facing the stand of timber. The house itself sat back against the sheer edge of a rocky hill, so approach from that direction, while possible, would be difficult. He should be able to spot most of them coming from the windows.

Most of them. Probably not all of them.

"This is your doing!" Lorine shouted at the old woman. "You brought this down on us with all your talk of visions and cures, you wicked old bitch!"

Mother Agnes regarded her silently, scowling. Lorine was livid with anger, her hair damp with sweat against her face, and she approached the old woman with hands raised, as if to grab her and choke her down.

"You, girl," the old woman said. "You gone against your own people, taking up with this gunman. You're letting the instinct to rut rule over your head and move you off from where you ought to be."

"You don't know anything," Lorine said. "You don't know what it's like, living with them. They cuff you and kick you and then try and drag you off in the brush and put their hands all over you. They all tried it, even that sick old man, but I never let them."

"You best take stock, girl. This'll go hard with you."

"I don't care. I've put an end to it now. They can kill me if they want, but they lost."

Mother Agnes looked at Julia. Julia had gone bone white, trembling as she stood there, hands to her mouth.

"You're the one they're after, woman," Mother Agnes said. "I seen you, I seen you was coming. I always know." Her old eyes were wide, belying her words, as though she were amazed to see Julia standing here, one of her prophesies made flesh. She took a couple of doddering steps toward her, one hand coming up to touch Julia's face, to test her, make certain she was real. Julia shrank back from her.

"I won't hurt you, dear. Come see Mother Agnes."

Slocum said to Lorine, "Get her out of here."

"I ain't leaving my own house," Mother Agnes said.

"They're headed here," Slocum said, "and they're going to come shooting. I'm not one to hold an old woman to be a shield for my bullets. You go out, and right now. If I have to I'll pick you up and toss you out to your own chickens."

"They'll kill you here, gunman. I already told you I seen it. I'm never wrong. You'll die here."

"Get out!" Lorine screamed. "Get out now!"

Slocum heard them coming through the trees, the crack of horses moving across dead branches in the timber, the shouts of the men from one to another. Any moment now should see them breaking into the yard. He grabbed the old woman by her bony arm and opened the door just wide enough for her.

"All due respect for your years, ma'am, but you're leaving. Go on out to them, halloo at them, so they see you."

"I'll be there when they bury you, gunman."

Slocum shoved her out, feeling her resist him even as he got her outside and past the door, the old sinews and muscles in her arm strong and wiry against his hand. He slammed the door behind her and grabbed up the Henry as a rider broke through the timber into the yard.

"Get down!" he shouted to Julia and Lorine, and heard them drop to the floor behind him.

They already knew he was here; now he had to demonstrate that he was serious about it. He aimed the Henry at the rider, the foolish man out there in the open, blinking in the sunlight and looking around, pistol uselessly out and pointed at nothing. Slocum fired, saw the man's chest tear open as he dropped from his horse to land, kicking and squirming, on the ground. The horse bolted and ran.

Immediately Slocum saw more movement within the trees, shadows of men on horseback, and others on foot lower down. He placed a couple rounds in there, saw one shadow go reeling, hit, and the rest retreat farther back into cover. Mother Agnes was out there now, deliberately placing herself in his line of fire as she walked toward her people, and Slocum held up. Her presence kept Deward's bunch from shooting as well, and he heard a hoarse shout informing all to hold their fire until she got clear.

There was movement behind him, and then suddenly Lorine was next to him. He heard the quick pant of her breath.

"Get back down."

"Give me a gun," she said. "I can shoot."

"No."

"You think I'm feeble? I can shoot and I'm here with you. Give me your pistol."

He realized the sense in her request. He gave her the Remington he'd taken from her dead cousin last night, and the canvas pouch containing the bullets and powder and caps. "You know how to reload that once it's empty?"

"I grew up loading pistols," she said. She laid the

barrel on the edge of the window, her eyes on the trees, and thumbed the hammer back. Slocum was pleased to see that she was calm and focused, not popping off shots uselessly, but waiting for a target.

They watched the edge of the timber and the shadows just beyond. They spotted an occasional blurring of movement, flits of color that were there and gone in the space of a second as men positioned themselves. Slocum wondered how many there were, and if they would rush the place.

"*Slocuuuumm!*"

Deward's voice, deep and booming from off to the right. Slocum squinted toward the sound, straining through slitted eyes to pierce the growth and catch sight of him.

"You best come out of there easy, Slocum! You and Lorine step on out and fetch that girl with you, and we won't bust no caps on you! Otherwise we're coming in to get you, and folks'll get hurt all around! You hear me?"

Slocum's eyes flicked from the right to the left. He spotted movement, low down among the trees. Lorine said, "Are you going to answer him?"

"I'll answer him all right," he said, and raised the rifle, fired, jacked in another round, fired again, and saw a man fling up his arms and turn, spinning.

It was a cue for general firing from the timber. Slocum and Lorine ducked down at the bursts of flame and white powder smoke, hearing the blasts and feeling the hollow thock of the bullets as they plowed into the logs of the cabin. Bullets zipped through the windows and smashed into the wall behind them. Crockery exploded.

"Oh, John!" Julia wailed. "They're coming!"

It was a cry of despair and helplessness. She lay crumpled on the floor, her hair in the dirt and her hands over her face, but her eyes were still visible, wide and unblinking through her splayed fingers. Her body jerked with the sound of each gunshot, as if she were taking the bullets herself. Slocum had seen cases of the same paralyzing fear in the War. Some people weren't meant to go through such things—certainly not a financier's daughter from Chicago.

Nor the dirt-poor half sister of a chinless killer, but Lorine was there at the window. She raised the Remington and fired, cocked it and fired again.

She said, "John—?"

"I see them," Slocum said, and raised the Henry and fired, and again, and twice more. Two groups of Deward's men broke on either side of them, running, shooting, three men in each bunch, heading for the sides of the house. Slocum saw two catch his bullets and fall, but one man dove for a water barrel just at the edge of Slocum's vision, rolled and was gone. He saw another man go down under Lorine's gun, but then the pistol was empty, and two more men disappeared around the opposite edge of the house.

There were no windows around the sides of the cabin, no back door, and there was no fire in the hearth for them to use by covering the chimney to smoke them out—but the house was surrounded now.

Lorine set to frantic work reloading the Remington, her hands shaking. She spilled powder and dropped the lead pistol balls on the floor. She scrambled for them, scooping them up in her fingers.

Slocum fired twice more as another group broke from the trees, led by a stout, bearded man he thought at first was Deward. But the man was too short to be

Deward, and Slocum blasted a hole in his belly and sent him staggering backward against the stubbled bark of a pine, where the man sat down and died quickly with his eyes open. The other two men dove back for cover, Slocum's bullets chewing the dust behind their heels.

Only a matter of time now. He heard the men at the sides of the house, and he knew there was only one thing they could be doing, only one logical move: They would set fire to the cabin and burn them out into the open.

He wondered if he could kill the women himself before it was over, if he could do it. Shoot them to keep them from whatever would come after he was dead, when Deward and Bobby Todd got their hands on them. A quick bullet behind the ear would be better, cleaner.

He heard the kerosene come down the chimney.

A trickle at first, and the thought that struck him was ridiculous, that one of the men had climbed onto the roof to urinate down the chimney, and then the trickle became a whoosh and the kerosene flooded the fireplace, covering the ashes and spilling out on the floor beyond the hearth. A moment later came the low percussive whump as the man dropped a match and the kerosene burst to life, illuminating the interior of the cabin and reflecting sudden eerie light back from the blue-and-green glass bottles of potions and herbs on Mother Agnes's shelves.

Lorine dropped the pistol and jumped for the fireplace, grabbing a blanket from the small pallet in the corner that was Mother Agnes's bed. She slapped at the flames.

"Get up and help me!" she shouted at Julia. "Do you want to die in here? Get up!"

Julia lay there for a moment longer, then turned to watch Lorine fight the fire. She got to her feet, her face blank, stumbled to the pallet for another blanket and joined Lorine.

They beat at the flames, but it was useless. The initial burst of kerosene had burned quickly off, but the flames had caught the tinder-dry bureau and leapt to the shelves and to the paper glued as insulation on the inside wall, and in seconds the entire side of the house was ablaze. Slocum stayed at the window, firing whenever he saw movement, but the movement out there had largely ceased. They were still in the trees, but now they were waiting, watching. He heard the pop and the crack from outside, from both sides of the house, and he knew they had scattered more kerosene around the base of the walls out there and set it afire. Soon the whole cabin would be a ball of flame.

"I tried, John!" Lorine called, still slapping futilely with the blanket. "I really tried!"

"I know you did, girl," Slocum said.

"They're going to win!"

The flames climbed the walls and caught at the muslin sheet that served as a ceiling. A spindly chair burst alight, and Lorine kicked it over and away. She retreated. Slocum felt the sweat roll down his chest and back and beneath his arms, and he remembered the feral look of anticipation on Bobby Todd's face when Slocum had hung wristbound from the tree and the flames had licked at his boots, and he knew there was just such a look there now as Bobby Todd crouched among the trees and watched the cabin consume itself.

The smoke thickened. His eyes burned. When he turned to look at the women, they were obscured in a grayish white haze. Lorine coughed hard, and again.

The moment was thundering toward them, and Slocum knew he would do what there was to do. Surrendering the women to Deward and the others was unthinkable. Lorine would die and Julia they would use for their own warped goals, and if they did not kill her when they were through, her mind would be shattered.

"Down on the floor!" he shouted. "Down on your faces, flat down!"

Lorine started to obey, then stopped and looked at Julia. She pointed at Slocum. "You'd best put your arms around his neck, and kiss him and thank him, because he's about to give it all for you. It ain't going to work, and they're going to kill him, any minute now, but you'd best know before it's over what he's done!"

That said, Lorine lay down on the floor. To await the bullet. She began to cry, quietly, breathing through her open mouth, coughing, eyes clamped shut.

Julia looked at Slocum, and for a moment he was certain she was going to come to him, and he didn't know what to feel about it—though it wasn't going to make a hell of a lot of difference in a minute or so. The heat in the cabin was becoming unbearable, raking his skin.

Julia rushed for the door, flung it open and ran out into the yard.

"*No!*" Slocum shouted.

She ran to the middle of the yard, and a few shots thunked into the cabin walls, sent by overanxious shooters ready to fire at the first movement seen, and then Deward's voice came strong and hard: "Hold your damn fire! Anybody shoots that woman is a dead man!"

The firing ceased immediately.

Julia lifted her arms, hands up and out. "Stop this!" she shouted. "Let them alone! Here I am!"

19

Bobby Todd grinned, as if pleased at the chance to see Slocum once again. His pale blue eyes were red-rimmed from powder smoke. "Let's kill him now, Deward. I'll do it. One right above the nose."

Deward said, "You'll get your chance, boy. But not just yet, not unless he moves real stupid."

Bobby Todd gave a short burst of laughter. "He ain't about to do that." He waggled his pistol. "Down on your knees, Slocum, so I ain't got to work so hard to watch you. Do it, now—and you too, Lorine, goddamn you. Get down there on your knees."

Slocum looked around him and saw too many guns and too many unfriendly faces. The men, seven of them, including the two remaining Halsey brothers, all stared at him with hard, cold eyes. The only emotion apparent in them was a grim resolve.

They had come out of the trees gradually, hesitating even after Slocum had stepped out and laid down his weapons. It was as if they were still suspicious of him, still edgy. The bodies of their kin lay scattered here

169

and there around them where Slocum's bullets had cut them down.

Behind them, the old woman's cabin was fully engulfed, a roaring hell out of which Slocum and the women had emerged, knowing that the hell they faced now could be worse.

He got slowly to his knees. Bobby Todd kicked at Lorine to hurry her along as she kneeled. She cried out and fell forward onto her hands. Slocum jerked and lunged, but Bobby Todd's pistol barrel jabbed into his neck.

"Now, now. Behave yourself," Bobby Todd said. "Boom, boom," he added, and lifted the barrel as if in recoil, then laughed again.

Deward stepped slowly around Julia, one big hand on her arm, looking her up and down. "You ain't hurt, are you, woman? I don't see no blood on you nowheres."

Julia did not answer. She stood with head lowered and arms down at her sides. Her eyes were clamped shut, her lips pressed tightly together as if ready for a massive blow to strike her, braced for it, waiting. Her face was dirty and stained with smoke, except for the wet trails where tears had streaked.

Deward stepped over to where Lorine knelt. She stared up at him, unwavering. Deward opened his mouth as if to say something, then abandoned any such effort and backhanded her, a vicious blow that rocked her head sideways. Slocum moved, but Bobby Todd's gun was still pressed to the side of his neck. Deward slapped Lorine once more, then turned and stepped away, shaking his head.

Somebody brought the horses up from the trees.

Deward grabbed his reins and swung into the saddle, then unlimbered his pistol from his holster.

"I only want two men," he said, and pointed. "You and you. Come along and keep your rifles pointed at this son of a bitch here while we fetch them all to the house. The rest of you go on home. Your part in this is done. Gather up your dead kin, take them home and lay them out proper."

The two men Deward had pointed out came over and helped get Slocum and Lorine to their feet while the rest of the crowd dwindled off, back toward the bodies of their dead. Bobby Todd gave Lorine a shove, and she stumbled forward, almost losing her balance.

"You know the way, girl. You get to walking toward home."

"It ain't going to work, Deward," Lorine said. "You might as well give it up right now."

"You let me worry about what's going to work and what ain't," Deward said.

They started walking, Slocum and Lorine in the lead, Julia just behind, and the four mounted men driving them like cattle.

"Why we bothering to fetch these other two back for, Deward?" Bobby Todd whined. "They's just extra baggage. Oughta drop them and have it done with."

"They fought against it," Deward said, "I want them to stand there and see it. I want to prove to them it weren't any use to fight us."

The yard of the Halsey place was peaceful after the noise and smoke and confusion of the morning. The chickens still fussed in the dirt, and the hogs still rooted in their pen. The door to the house stood open a crack.

Deward reined up and looked at the two men who had ridden along. "You boys can go on now. The rest of this is private family business."

The two men nodded and sheathed their weapons. They looked uneasy, as if anxious to be gone from there. One of the men looked at Slocum and spat grimly on the ground.

"When you kill this one, put a ball in him for me," he said.

"It'll get done," Deward said in a solemn tone. "It'll all get done now. Ain't nothing can stop it."

The men rode off, perhaps to join the others. Deward stepped down from his saddle, walked to the front door and kicked it wide open. He covered Slocum and the women with his pistol while Bobby Todd dismounted, then jerked his head toward the house.

"All right, get on in there." He took hold of Julia's arm and shoved her inside.

Bobby Todd prodded Slocum and Lorine in after her. Slocum entered and immediately began scanning the walls and shelves for a weapon of any sort, anything he might use to beat or stab, but there was nothing. Lorine moved slowly, dragging her bare feet against the swept dirt floor, her face tense. She looked straight ahead.

They moved to the curtained area behind which lay the gray and motionless old man. His head was flat against the pillow, his mouth partly open. His eyes were closed.

"Bobby Todd," Deward said, "you keep that son of a bitch covered while this happens."

"I got him," Bobby Todd said, jabbing Slocum in the ribs with his pistol.

"Now you're going to see, Slocum," Deward said. "You're going to see I was right."

"What I'm going to see is you ruin somebody on the word of an ignorant, superstitious old woman," Slocum said.

"You're going to see I was right!" Deward shouted. "And then you're going to die." He pointed his pistol at Julia, wagging it like a finger. "You, girl. You're going to get in bed and minister to that old man the way you would minister to your husband. Get peeled down. Now."

She was trying not to cry, Slocum could see. Slowly she began to unbutton her dress. She gave Slocum one final look of longing, then closed her eyes, as if to hide what was happening from herself if from no one else.

Slocum felt the pistol barrel ease from against his ribs, just barely, and he knew Bobby Todd would be watching Julia with open-mouthed eagerness. He wondered how good the man's reflexes were, what kind of chance there was.

Joshua Halsey lay still and blank, his mouth still open, showing a row of snaggled, discolored teeth, and the teeth were dry in the close air of the cabin.

The teeth were dry . . .

"Stop," Lorine said. Her voice was bold enough to draw Deward's attention from Julia's open dress.

Slocum had already seen what must have happened, a flash of knowledge that was suddenly there. *The teeth were dry.* Even a sick man licked his lips. Even a sick man would have the wet glint of saliva on his teeth.

"Stop it, Deward," Lorine said. "Leave her alone. He's dead."

For the first time since they entered the room, Deward turned and really looked at the wasted old man in the bed, at the gray pallor and gaping mouth, at the covers that failed to rise and fall. He laid a huge, black-haired hand on the old man's forehead, jerked it back, then laid it on again and left it there. Feeling the coolness and realizing what it meant.

"Daddy?" he said, his voice high and disbelieving. "You can't be dead, Daddy. It ain't supposed to be happening like that."

Then he saw the small puddle of red on the floor, under the toe of his boot, the blood that had run from beneath the covers to drip down and soak into the smooth, bare floor.

He gave out a roar and flung the covers back.

Joshua Halsey had not bled much before he died, but enough to mark the stab wounds—two of them, high up, around the heart.

Deward lifted his head and bellowed his anger up and out into the sky.

"*Nooo*!"

"God almighty," Bobby Todd said. "He's been stuck."

Deward glared at Lorine, his face dark with rage. "You done this, you little bitch!"

"Yes, I done it," Lorine said, glaring defiantly back at him. "I done it this morning right after you left. I done it so you'd stop all this meanness—so you'd leave these people alone."

Deward shot her twice in the belly, and Lorine slammed back against the wall, knocking a tarnished CSA medal from its shelf. She clutched at herself, her mouth closed tightly, taking it, having known it was coming, and Slocum gave a yell and moved, but Bobby Todd's hand clamped down hard on his arm and the pistol barrel dug into his ribs.

She died in seconds, her hands falling away from the wounds and the breath coming out of her in a final, rushing sigh, but Deward did not wait to see it. He grabbed a handful of Julia's dark hair and twisted.

"By God, woman, you'll do me, then!"

He holstered his pistol and continued to twist, forcing Julia to her knees. He fumbled at the buttons of his pants.

Bobby Todd's eyes glittered with the realization of what was happening. "Deward," he said, "Deward, you hold on, big brother, you leave a little bit for me, you hear?" He leaned forward, his dead father forgotten, his dead sister forgotten, and he was grinning.

Slocum lunged.

He grabbed the pistol in his right hand and twisted, coming in hard with his left fist. He caught Bobby Todd in the middle of his weasel face. Bobby Todd yelped as he went down, and Slocum wrenched the pistol from him, gave it a flip and caught it solidly in his hand. Deward turned, still gripping Julia's hair, his pants open and his swollen penis projecting from it. He clawed at his pistol. Slocum shot him in the throat, and saw the blood erupt in a steaming geyser, and shot him again, driving him backward to careen off the bed and against the wall and slump down, sliding into a sitting position, his eyes already glazing over.

Bobby Todd came at him with a howl, and Slocum dodged backward to see the gleaming arc of the knife slice the air inches from his chest. He tried to bring the gun in, to center on the man's chest, but he was too close, and as Bobby Todd lunged again, he raised his left arm to block the knife and felt the hilt bang into his wrist. The man's hot animal breath was in his face. He shoved. Bobby Todd stumbled back, shouting word-lessly, and came in again. Slocum shot him through the forehead, spraying the wall behind him with blood and brains as the back of the man's skull disintegrated with the exit of the bullet.

It was over. The gray smell of powder smoke was thick in the room. Julia had slumped down next to the bed, her face covered with her hands, lying on her side and trying to draw herself up into a ball. She cried out when Slocum touched her, and flinched away.

"It's all right, Julia," he said. "They can't hurt you now. Let's get you out of this room."

After a moment she allowed Slocum to help her to her feet, but she kept her head down and her eyes squeezed shut. He led her into the big kitchen and placed her in a chair. Then he knelt down and held her, the pistol still hot in his hand, while she cried.

20

They rode together on Bobby Todd's horse, and no one bothered them. Perhaps it was because the people on the mountain could not imagine that the Halseys might be beaten, and so did not look for the lean, black-haired man to go riding away with the girl.

She lay heavy against his chest, clutching the saddle horn with both hands. She did not speak; nor had she made a sound since she'd finished crying in Lorine's kitchen. Slocum's arms cradled her as his hands held the reins. Every so often she shuddered against him.

There were only two things left to do.

Mr. Conway met them on the front porch of the Garrison House. He and a couple of grizzled bar patrons helped Julia down from the saddle. The smell of whiskey was strong on Conway's breath.

"Is she hurt? Should we fetch a doctor for her? Slocum, I'll tell you now, if they did anything to injure my daughter—"

Slocum stepped down, raised a fist and punched Conway hard in the center of the chest. It was a means of getting the man's attention, and it was enough to send Conway back three steps. His face went slack with astonishment.

"She's not hurt, Conway," Slocum said. "Just shook up pretty bad. But there isn't any doctor to go fetch, because you traipsed over to his house last night and led those people there, and that got him killed. He's dead because you did exactly what I told you not to do."

"Now listen just a minute—" Conway sputtered.

"No. You listen. You take this girl upstairs and put her to bed, and then you sit next to her and hold onto her hand. You move an inch away from her, and I'll find out about it. You won't like what will happen."

Conway's eyes glittered with anger, but he attempted to smooth his ruffled dignity. "Look here, Slocum, I know what you've done for us has been—"

"I did what there was to do. But there wouldn't have been quite so much if you'd been the kind of father she needed."

He waited, knowing that if Conway opened his mouth again, he would strike him, knock him down and hope it would jar some sense into the man's thick head. He half hoped it would happen, and at the same time he knew it would not be a good thing for Julia to see.

But Conway wilted. His eyes fell. He turned, took a gentle hold on Julia's arm and led her into the hotel. Slocum watched them go.

Now for the rest of it. The final thing.

He turned to one of the bar patrons, a white-haired man who had hovered close by on the hotel porch, listening. "You," he said. "The Marshal showed back up yet?"

The man, blinking, gave a quick, jerking nod. "Yessir, he did. He was in his office this morning, skulking around at the window."

"You go see him. You tell him that Deward Halsey and his brothers are dead. Tell him John Slocum will be waiting for him in Collins's saloon."

The man nodded, and scuttled away.

Slocum went down the street to Collins's place, the narrow saloon that had been the site of Reed's provocation and murder of the drunken teamster—how long ago? Two days, three? It seemed longer than that. He stepped smoothly through the slatted doors and then took a light step to the side so that he would not be silhouetted in the doorway.

Four customers at the bar. Only one of them, a burly cowhand, was armed, and when he saw Slocum, he finished his drink and walked out. The bartender stood with both hands on the counter and watched Slocum. It was not Collins, but some man who worked for him.

Slocum said, "Whiskey. In the bottle. And one glass."

It was provided. Slocum took the bottle and glass and, holding them in his left hand, moved to the center of the room and seated himself against the wall so that he had a good view of the front entrance, and of the narrow doorway leading out to the trash-strewn alley in the rear. He leaned back in his chair, poured a drink and downed it, feeling the whiskey burn a path down his throat to his belly, where it hit and expanded, flooding him with warmth. He poured another and let it sit on the table in front of him. He waited. He doubted that it would be a long wait.

Reed would have to come. If he was to retain any part of his standing in this town, and his dignity as a man, he would have to face Slocum and kill him. Slocum had destroyed his family. And last night in the canyon Slocum had seen him turn and run. That could make a man hate another like nothing else.

It was five minutes or so before the commotion began in the street outside—the rapid clump of boots on the plank sidewalk, boots belonging to people eager to be elsewhere in a hurry. Slocum saw figures whip past the doors, women hurrying children ahead of them. Someone mounted a horse and spurred it away at a gallop.

He heard shouting. Someone said, "He's got a shotgun!"

He checked the area around him and made certain it was clear in case he had to move fast.

"*Slocum!*"

In the street outside. Slocum raised the drink in his left hand and sipped half of it down. His feet were flat on the floor. He did not answer.

"Slocum!" Reed hollered, his voice strained and breaking. "You come out here, Slocum, give yourself up, and there won't be no cause for trouble! We'll wait and talk to the sheriff together, see if we can't straighten everything out!"

Slocum smiled at the prospect. Not very damn likely.

"Slocum! I mean it! Don't make me come in there after you!"

Come, Slocum thought.

The remaining customers, and the bartender with them, banged their way out the back door, leaving Slocum to his fate. Slocum downed the rest of his drink, allowing Reed to sweat out there in the street, figuring it would take only one long minute more before the man broke and opened the ball.

It came with a rush. The rapid crunch of Reed's

boots in the dirt of the street, two hollow clumps as he hit the boardwalk, and then Reed burst in through the batwing doors, Reed with a face drained of color, eyes wide and on fire and his mouth tight, and in his hands the double-barreled greener. Slocum left his chair and dove to the right as Reed fired, the roar deafening in the narrow room. The blast smashed the back of the chair and took the bottle with it, peppering the wall with shot and splinters and an amber spray of whiskey. Slocum rolled to the left, got his feet under him and dove again as the second shot came, Reed hurried and frantic and firing too quickly, the charge ripping the air where Slocum had been. Reed threw the shotgun away as if it were a vile thing, empty and useless and beyond contempt. He clawed for the pistols in the sash at his waist.

Slocum drew. He shot Reed once in the chest, saw the white shirt jump with the impact of the bullet. Reed staggered, his expression changing from frantic anger to disbelief. His right gun was drawn, but his left hand fell limply to his side, then fumbled at the buttons of his shirt as if to free whatever had gotten in there. He raised the pistol, cocked it, stumbled back two steps. Slocum shot him again, and saw a tiny black hole appear high on the man's left cheek, a black speck as if an insect had suddenly landed there, and then Reed's eyes went blank and sightless and he fell back through the slatted doors to land on the boardwalk with his booted feet still inside.

Slocum holstered his pistol, went around the bar and found a fresh bottle of whiskey—good stuff, a labeled brand. He poured himself a shot and downed it, then poured another and stood there until his breathing slowed.

• • •

He purchased a horse from the liveryman for a reasonable price and readied his tack for a long ride. He had been headed for Wyoming before this thing started, and he figured to continue heading that way. He'd see if those cattlemen on the Powder River still needed him. The cook at the hotel made him up a bag of sandwiches and sold him two pounds of coffee beans and a side of bacon, wrapped in cheesecloth, which he secured in his saddlebags. He had tobacco and gunpowder and lead. He took a bath in the room behind the Garrison barbershop, and shaved. He suspected the sheriff would arrive no earlier than tomorrow morning, and Slocum did not plan to be there to meet him. There was no easy way to explain what had happened.

Mr. Conway was seated next to the bed in his vest and shirtsleeves when Slocum came in. Julia lay with her hair fanned out on the clean white pillow. Her eyes were closed, but her features were relaxed and there was good color in her cheeks.

Her eyes opened when she heard him enter.

"John—"

Conway got up and met him halfway, extending his hand. Slocum did not acknowledge the gesture, and after a moment Conway lowered his hand and stepped back.

"Mr. Slocum, she told me what you did, and of course everyone's heard about the Marshal, the fact that he was in cahoots with those—"

"I didn't come to rehash anything," Slocum said.

"No, of course not," Conway said, and cleared his throat. "I suppose it's the money." He reached into his vest and pulled out a billfold. "I guess no one can say you didn't earn it—"

"I don't want your damn money either."

Conway blinked. "I made the offer, and I stand by it."

"It's blood money. My hands are stained bad enough as it is."

"I got justice. I insist you take what you earned."

From the bed, Julia said, "Shut up, Dad. Don't make a bigger fool of yourself than you already have."

Slocum said, "Get out of here a minute. I want a few words with your daughter alone."

"I hardly think that's proper given her condition . . ."

His voice trailed off under Slocum's stare, and in a moment he nodded, quietly left the room and closed the door behind him.

Slocum sat down beside the bed and took Julia's hand. She squeezed it and smiled up at him. The tiny lines at the corners of her eyes were deeper, and there was a weariness around her mouth.

"You don't think much of my father, do you?"

He smiled at her in what he hoped was a reassuring way. "It don't matter what I think. What counts is how you're doing."

"I'm all right. It'll take me a while to get over it, but I'll live. I'll survive."

"Whatever I did, it pales alongside of you stepping out of that cabin and giving yourself up. You did it to keep them from killing me, and I want you to know I realize it."

"That doesn't make us even," she said. "It doesn't come close."

"You're not going to have a bad time over this, are you?"

"You don't have to be concerned, John. I'm not going to close myself up in my room again. I'm not going to shut myself away. It was different this time. I had a man I cared about standing up for me, a man who didn't let me down."

He sat and held her hand. Outside, Wyoming waited, and he would get there. For now, while her father waited out in the hallway, he sat with her and held her hand.

JAKE LOGAN
TODAY'S HO'TTEST ACTION
WESTERN!